Scissors, Sisters & Manic Panics

Also by Ellie Phillips

Dads,
Geeks
& Blue
Haired
Freaks

Scissors, Sisters & Manic Panics

ELLIE PHILLIPS

First published in Great Britain in 2013
by Electric Monkey, an imprint of Egmont UK Limited
The Yellow Building, 1 Nicholas Road, London W11 4AN

Text copyright © 2013 Ellie Phillips
The moral rights of the author have been asserted

ISBN 978 1 4052 5820 3

1 3 5 7 9 10 8 6 4 2

www.electricmonkeybooks.co.uk

A CIP catalogue record for this title is available from the British Library

Typeset by Avon DataSet Ltd, Bidford on Avon, Warwickshire
Printed and bound in Great Britain by CPI Group

48755/1

EGMONT

Our story began over a century ago, when seventeen-year-old Egmont Harald Petersen found a coin in the street. He was on his way to buy a flyswatter, a small hand-operated printing machine that he then set up in his tiny apartment.

The coin brought him such good luck that today Egmont has offices in over 30 countries around the world. And that lucky coin is still kept at the company's head offices in Denmark.

One for the girls: Bette, Jo, Tilly & Gail, and
'The Writing Ladies of the Royal Festival Hall'

1

Manic Panic

It is essential for the hairdresser (or barber) to have a part-time apprenticeship, at least one day a week, in a registered salon.
Guideline 1: Thames Gateway Junior Apprentice Hairdresser (or Barber) of the Year Award

I was having a bad hair day when this whole thing started.

Up until that point everything had been pretty peachy. I mean, I'd been feeling like my life was totally sorted for once: I had a cool boyfriend, I had a dad-type figure in my life who actually listened to me *and* I was following my ambition to be a greatass hairdresser. Unfortunately this last bit meant working every Saturday in my Aunt Lilah's salon – which was where the bad hair day came in and everything in my life went BANG . . .

That Saturday began as it always did, with Aunt Lilah yelling at me for not sweeping up the hair right. How can you criticise someone *for the way they're sweeping*?

'For the fifteenth time, Sadie, sweep the floor from left to right.'

'I am.'

'No, you're the wrong way round – from left to right facing the back door. That's the way the floor tilts. If you go the other way it's uphill and the draft comes under the door and blows the hair all over the salon again.'

'Yeah, it does do that actually. It blows all over the salon,' repeated Tiffany, who's so dumb that it's like the wheel's spinning but the hamster's dead.

Tiffany's the junior stylist who Aunt Lilah employs solely so that she has someone to bitch and complain at all the other days of the week when I'm not there. Saturday is Tiffany's day off from Aunt Lilah's bitching and she spends it repeating whatever Aunt Lilah's just said to me.

'Left to right.'

'Yes, Aunty.'

'Yeah, you gotta do it left to right.'

'Thanks, Tiffany.'

2

And it went on from there as usual.

'That's the wrong mug.'

'The wrong brush.'

'The wrong setting on the drier.'

'The wrong rollers.'

'The wrong sized pot.'

'The wrong gown.'

Wrong wrong wrong wrong wrong.

'Sorry, Aunty.'

'Yeah, it is wrong actually.'

'Whateva, Tiffany.'

It's not like I wasn't grateful to Aunty and all for making me Girl Saturday in her salon. Hair is, after all, my 'thing'. I was doing Level 1 Hairdressing at college one day per week, plus I was taking things to the next level in *World of Hairdressing* by entering the Thames Gateway Junior Apprentice Hairdresser (or Barber) of the Year Award – and all this on top of going to school. It was hard work, but I'm not lying when I say that I was loving it. I was flying! Except for Saturdays, when I was in Aunty's shop and I was not flying at all. I was stuck on the runway with no prospect whatsoever of a take-off.

At three thirty that Saturday Mrs Nellist came in for

her cut-and-colour while Aunty and Tiffany were out the back having a coffee and a Kit Kat, leaving me to sweep up from left to right as you're facing the back door, and that's kind of where everything got really ugly.

It was the hairstyle that Mrs Nellist never knew she wanted. That's all it was about. I don't know why everyone had to go so completely hysterical about it, but that's my family for you.

I think it was maybe the colour. In a certain light I'll admit that when she came out from under the dryer, Mrs Nellist's hair did look a little bit pink. I swear to God on a stack of Holy Bibles that it was not intentional. I'd tried out the tiniest smidgen of one of the new Manic Panic shades I'd been wanting to use for the longest time. Manic Panic do dayglo colours – like Fuschia Shock, Vampire Red and Electric Lemon. None of Aunt Lilah's customers would ever be up for any of those, being that they're all over thirty-five years of age and say things like, 'Oooh, I'm going to really be daring and go a shade lighter' or 'I want something radical: two millimetres off the top. It's going to be a whole new me.'

I don't know why Aunty had even bought the Manic Panic range. I think she got overwhelmed at the

4

Hair Show and thought she was running a completely different kind of salon, with interesting customers wanting to try out new looks and styles – which is the kind of salon I'd like to run one day. Anyway, in Aunt Lilah's salon I was banned from even suggesting Manic Panic in case it induced a heart attack or something, but this colour was called Pearly Queen, so it sounded like it was going to blend beautifully with Mrs Nellist's white curls – just pep them up a teensy bit. Plus Mrs Nellist was well up for it.

'I think it sounds nice, Sadie love,' she said when I suggested we try a new colour. 'I'm a secret smoker, y'know, and sometimes I think it makes me hair go a little bit yellow.'

Glamorous world, hairdressing. I'd had a Saturday job for twelve weeks in Aunt Lilah's shop and so far I'd seen dandruff, nits, seborrhoeic dermatitis (which is like mega-dandruff) and alopecia (this woman was literally bald on one side – it was like a nightmare).

So anyway, back to Mrs Nellist and her Colour by Nicotine. *Secret* smoker? Who was she kidding? I don't think I've ever seen Mrs Nellist without a ciggie in her hand. Even when she comes in the salon she has to nip out from under the dryer for a fly fag in the back garden.

So I did Pearly Queen because Mrs Nellist seemed enthusiastic, and I partly blame the ceiling in Aunt Lilah's salon for the result. It's a sort of blancmange pink, so with hindsight I think it was just the newly dyed glossy whiteness of Mrs Nellist's hair reflecting the ceiling colour that made everyone get a bit over-excited. I wish I'd pointed that out at the time. But what with Aunt Lilah shouting at me and turning on all the water jets and offering to rinse and strip the hair down for Mrs Nellist, and Tiffany repeating whatever Aunt Lilah had just said, it was kind of hard to think, let alone speak.

Tiffany, who is like living proof that evolution can go in reverse, made Mrs Nellist four cups of tea in a row, which made her go jittery, and she had to take one of her pills and they spilled all over the floor, and then I had to pick them up and count them and I kept coming out with different totals, which made her a bit upset. So then we had to calm her down with a camomile infusion which she said smelled of wee and made her feel even weirder. Aunt Lilah resorted to brandy then and this seemed to do the trick.

All the while Aunt Lilah was hissing and stage

whispering at me over the water jets. Mrs Nellist is very deaf so you don't actually have to hiss, and it was just annoying and unnecessary.

'And you've cut it too short, Sadie. She likes it jaw-length – *jaw-length*! It's barely past her ears!'

'But it suits her – she has such a little face, she can wear it short,' I said, which is true actually cos Mrs Nellist does look like a pixie, with a little pointy chin and a bony schnozz.

'Yes! But she doesn't want it short. She wants it jaw-length! You have to give the customers what they want.'

'How do you know she wants it jaw-length? She never said.'

This was true as well. I'd kept right on trimming while Aunty and Tiffany were in the back garden chomping through the Kit Kats and Mrs Nellist was saying, 'Yes, lovely dear. That's lovely.' She never once said, 'Stop!'

'Because she always wants it jaw-length!' continued Aunt Lilah, who was now manically whisking powder bleach and peroxide in a bowl like Gordon bloody Ramsay on Ritalin. 'Mrs Nellist has been coming to me for fourteen years and she has always had her hair JAW-LENGTH!'

You see, this is where Aunt Lilah and I fundamentally differ. As anyone who's heard my philosophy on haironomics will know, I firmly believe that you don't just give the customer the style they think they want or the style they've always had – because often they don't have a clue. You give them the style *they never knew they wanted*. It's like magic. It's like you can read their minds. I know this because I've tried it out on Mum, on my cousin Billy and on my boyfriend Tony – and with 100 per cent success, though I say so myself. I'd really like to try it out on Abe now that we're getting to know one another. Abe is my biological dad, who Billy and I tracked down last year. Unlike the rest of my family (Mum, Aunt Lilah, Uncle Zé, Great Aunty Rita) Abe actually listens to me. He is also undoubtedly in need of a decent haircut and I think I could be the person to give it to him. I truly believe that I can 'channel' hairstyles like psychics can read minds.

Personally I think that Mrs Nellist liked the hairstyle I gave her. She did leave the salon eventually, although only after she'd been to the toilet twice because of all the cups of tea. We didn't charge her for her hair and she was ever so pleased and really confused about why we'd washed her hair quite so many times . . . And then Aunt Lilah sent Tiffany home and made my Uncle Zé come downstairs for backup.

And then she fired me.

At first I thought she was joking.

'You're joking, right?' I said and laughed, although I didn't think she was being particularly funny.

But Aunt Lilah was not laughing.

'No really, I don't like to have to do this, Sadie, you being family and all, but it's the only way you'll learn to stay in line. You're a loose cannon and I can't afford to have you running riot in here with my customers once a week.'

Stay in line.

Running riot.

Loose cannon.

I tell you, my Aunt Lilah is power mad. She even sounds like some crazed military dictator rather than the owner of a crap salon in E9. She was standing there firing me in a pair of red spiked heels, with her eyebrows drawn on at an evil tilt. No wonder Uncle Zé says she reminds him of Imelda Marcos, who's this power-mad shoe-mad politician from the Philippines, which is where Uncle's from. The thing is, Uncle Zé has been married to Aunt Lilah for twenty-five years, so it's kind of a weird thing to say about the woman you love.

'You don't want me to come back next Saturday?' I said, swallowing hard, because a wave of panic was sweeping over me. Maybe it wasn't just panic. Actual tears were stinging my eyes. My hands shook like they always do when I am nervous or shocked. I felt as if I had never mucked up quite so badly. I felt ashamed of myself. Like I'd been too confident, conceited, arrogant – and I'd tripped myself up. Like when you're walking along the street in your best heels thinking you look so fine and then you twist your ankle for no reason. I had bombed myself out.

You'd think I'd be a teensy bit relieved wouldn't you? After all, there would be no more Saturdays dragging by in Aunt Lilah's salon, no more moan-ins with Tiffany, no more instructions about which way to sweep the floor. But being fired screwed my master plan, which was to win the Thames Gateway Junior Apprentice Hairdresser (or Barber) of the Year Award. I'd set my heart on it, and the main requirement was a part-time apprenticeship in a local salon. And I'd just lost mine.

'But I need the job, Aunty . . .' I said. A tear started to spill. I trapped it with my knuckle.

'Well you should have thought of that, Sadie Nathanson, before you dyed Mrs Nellist's hair pink. No, I think it's best if we draw a line under this,' said Aunty, and she started sweeping up from left to right facing the back door so that the hair went downhill and when the wind blew it didn't go all over the shop.

2

Pancit With Tears

The hairdresser (or barber) should remain calm and professional at all times, ensuring that best practice in customer relations is observed.

Guideline 2: Thames Gateway Junior Apprentice Hairdresser (or Barber) of the Year Award

Uncle Zé said he thought being fired would be the making of me. He took me next door to his café and gave me *pancit* with pork, which is one of his best 'cheering up' dishes.

'Your aunt doesn't mean to be fierce, *anak*, but you know what she's like. We all have to do what we're told. You know what? Everyone gets fired once in their lives. See it as an opportunity. You can have a fresh start — maybe somewhere you have a bit more freedom to try stuff out. Somewhere with younger customers maybe?'

He was right. Working at Delilah's wasn't like my

12

dream job or anything. It's not a particularly good salon, but I'm kind of fond of it. I have spent countless hours there. I know every inch, every chair and its quirks, every tap, every dryer. I probably took my first steps on that floor and I've played a million games on it too. When we were shorties, my cousin Billy and I would line up the mixing pots and the brushes and pretend that the Pot People were going into battle with the Brush People. I was on first-name terms with the curlers – I swear I knew every hairpin in the box. That salon had been my world for the longest time. It was my anchor. OMG – not to be too dramatic, but that salon was my *life* . . .

Two fat tears fell into my *pancit*.

'*Anak*, that dish has plenty salt as it is,' said Uncle. 'It needs something, but it's not salt.' Then he winked at me, which of course made me cry even more.

'Stop being so nice to me, *tito* – you're making it worse!' I pleaded.

'I'm your *tito*, my job is to make it worse,' said Uncle Zé.

Anyone who knows me knows that Uncle Zé is basically my dad. In fact there was a moment – last year, before I found Abe – when I thought that Uncle Zé actually *was* my dad. No, really! I began to think my mum had been lying to me all these years and that my 'dad' wasn't an anonymous sperm donor that she carefully chose off the Internet at all. I started to suspect that Uncle Zé was maybe more than just my uncle. At the time when I was having these suspicions my boyfriend Tony Cruz said my life was like something from the Mid West of America, where people find out that their cat is really their brother or whatever. My cousin Billy and I went on a crazy trail, hacking into Mum's PC looking for clues about my 'donor', and of course, the truth was far less twisted than I feared. My dad turned out to be a Mr Abraham Smith, Municipal Gardener from Bough Beeches, Kent.

So Abe is half of my genes – I like to think of him as the generous half. After all, it takes proper generosity to help someone to have a baby and not shout about it. If Aunt Lilah did something like that she'd expect a double page spread in *Heat* or *The Hackney Gazette* or something. But Abe is not like that. He's pretty chilled and his hands shake like mine do when he's nervous. This was practically the first thing I noticed when me and Mum went to meet up with him last October – a whole year ago now.

That meeting was a pretty special moment in my life, because even though Abe didn't exactly seem like my dad he did seem like a nice guy, and now that we've got to know each other better I can honestly say that he *is* a nice guy. When I see him he asks me loads of questions and then he *listens* to my answers! These are two things I am not used to. In my actual family, people ask you questions like, 'Do you think I deserve to be spoken to like that?' or 'Who died and made you Queen?' or, if it's Great Aunty Rita (my oldest known living relative), 'Do you have a nice Jewish boyfriend yet, *bubelah*?'

Abe asks me about my ambitions, about what I'm good at, my likes, my dislikes. Even his girlfriend Sarah talks to me like I'm an adult – like we're on a level. Sarah is pretty cool, but fussy about her hair, which is straight and thin and which she likes to hide behind. She's one of those people who's really really sensitive – like I bet she notices if you take a millimetre too much off her fringe. I was kind of honoured on my third visit to Bough Beeches when Sarah said I could do her hair. I think it was a big deal for her, and I made sure that I didn't screw up.

I shared my philosophy on hair with her and also my top tips on hairdresser-spotting, which are as follows:

1. Hairdressers often have things stuck to their clothing – like section clips or Kirby grips. That's because hairdressers need (but don't have) three hands; two to do the hair and an extra one with an elongated arm to take out the clips and put them in a box on the other side of the salon. Because we only have two hands we end up sticking the clips to ourselves and then forgetting we put them there until we're at a restaurant or a barmitzvah and a kind stranger points out that we've had a section grip stuck to the bottom of our jumper for the last hour, which members of our own family neglected to mention.

2. Hairdressers are often to be found asleep on the tube at about 8.30 p.m. on a Saturday night. Sometimes they're the people that wake up in the tube terminus at High Barnet or Amersham or other weird places you've never been to. You see Saturday is the busiest day of the week for a hairdresser. You stand up for ten hours cutting, washing and brushing other people's hair, and by closing up time you are a wreck. There's absolutely no chance you'll get up the energy to go out yourself.

That's why some hairdressing salons are like nightclubs, with loud music and crazy hair and clothes – because this is the substitute for a night out for a hard-working hairdresser. Actual hairdresser nights out usually occur on a Monday when the salon has been closed all day.

3. Hairdressers are acquaintance magnets. A hairdresser at a party may inspire a queue. Once the secret is out that you do hair you will never be entirely friendless, but unless you insist on charging for your services from the word 'go', you may end up penniless. So, if you see a tramp-woman with fabulous hair, the chances are she used to be a hairdresser. That's a bit like the 50p lady round our way; her clothes are always in tatters and she generally looks as if she's never eaten a square meal in her life, but every so often she gets her hair done and it's surprisingly chic. Someone told me she used to be a hairdresser and I believe them. It totally figures.

As I explained all this to Sarah, it did make me wonder why on earth I'd chosen this career in the first place. But the point is I have chosen it. And I am totally 100 per cent committed to it.

Well, Abe just sat and watched us while I was

cutting Sarah's hair and listened to me talk. He didn't interfere like your normal, real dad might – like Uncle Zé would, for example. You see I realised quite early on in our relationship that Abe might be my biological dad, but he was never going to be Dad. He's just Abe – he's like this extra relative I have who happens to be a nice guy. While I was cutting Sarah's hair he was a little nervous – his hands shook a bit. But my hands didn't shake while I was cutting because I am NOT nervous about hair. Because I know I'm good at it. At least, I thought I was until Aunt Lilah fired me.

Now Uncle was doing *his* 'dad' bit and picking up the pieces. He waved a tenner at me.

'You buy yourself a treat with that,' he said. 'Put it towards new clothes or something.'

'I can't, *tito*. I've just been fired. I don't deserve it.'

'Course you do; you work hard. I work hard, your Aunt Lilah works hard. We all work hard.' Then he stood up and said, 'That *pancit* needs more fish sauce,' before disappearing into the kitchen.

My phone buzzed. I stared at it. A text from Mum.

What happened?

18

I ignored it. The news had clearly taken less than a nanosecond to travel from Aunt Lilah to Mum. She'd be on her way round here.

I texted Billy, just so he could get my side of things before he got Aunty's.

Ur mum just fired me

Within seconds there were two texts back. One was from Billy.

No way wot you done?

And the other one was from my boyfriend – that's José Antonio de Cruz himself, or Tony Cruz to the general public. He'd have clocked the text I sent to Billy, being that they're best mates and generally hang out being geeky together.

Wossup?

Then the phone was ringing and Tony was on the end of it.

'Dish the dirt,' he said.

So I put on the brave face and mopped up the tears and told him all about it. About the hair and Mrs Nellist and the sweeping and Aunty. In the telling, my personal tragedy became a good anecdote and I could just imagine Tony's cute little head bobbing up and down. It's his nervous tick, but it also makes him like the most positive person I know. It used to annoy me, but now I find it kind of reassuring.

'Your aunt sounds as if she really lost it there,' he said. 'See – you should never work with your family.'

'She did lose it,' I said, 'and you were right about not working with family. Are you nodding your head off right now?'

'So what if I'm nodding my head – what is the problem with nodding my head?' His voice went up at the end like it always does when he's irritated. I like him even when he sounds like that.

'You are way, way too positive about life. It's not natural.'

'And you are way, way too angsty. Why are you so angsty?'

Why was I angsty?

'Two reasons. Number 1: I've just been fired. And number 2: Have you met my family at all?'

'Y'know,' said Tony, 'I think you badly need some TLC, maybe I'll swing by with Billy – see what you're up to . . .'

I knew exactly where this was leading, because Tony Cruz is always looking for an excuse to give me Tender Loving Care. Unfortunately, it is up to every member of my family to prevent him. And as my family live all over the neighbourhood, it means that my neighbourhood is a No Booty Mr Cutie zone.

As if on cue, there was a rapping sound on the glass of the café door. It was my mum. I rolled my eyes. Now I couldn't even have a *conversation* with Tony without being interrupted?

'Gotta go,' I said. 'Call you later.'

'Laters.'

Mum was mouthing *What happened?* at me through the door, like she couldn't even wait to be inside before starting to interrogate me. Oh God, why couldn't my family just give me a centimetre of space; a window of like five minutes to gather myself together before they turned everything into an episode of *Eastenders*?

Uncle came bustling through from the kitchen and opened the café door. '*Ay naku*, Angela, it's all fine. No drama here. We're just having a bite to eat. Join us if you like.'

Mum pulled up a chair and sat down at the table. Her hair needed a trim. Even though I totally remodelled her hair last year, making her ditch the two styles she'd always sported (one on the back and one on the front of her head), she never let me get at it regularly enough. It wasn't surprising that her hair had started to make its way back into the old shmullet. I made a mental note to pin her down to a trim at some point. Get her back into that stacked bob we'd gone for. But now didn't seem to be an appropriate moment.

Mum peered at me over her glasses while Uncle dished up *pancit*, for her this time. Then he went back into the kitchen, claiming to be hunting for the fish sauce again. He was giving us space. Subtle, my uncle.

'Are you OK? Do you want to talk about it?' said Mum.

'Not particularly, if that's all right with you.'

'That's OK. That's just fine.'

Her mouth went into a straight line. I was sure it

wasn't OK. I was sure that Mum was desperate to talk about it – that she was really frustrated that I didn't want to tell my side. Sure enough, five minutes into a conversation about other salons in the area who might be hiring, Mum said, 'But of course all salons will expect you to sweep up.'

'What's that supposed to mean?' I said.

'It's not supposed to mean anything,' said Mum.

'Has *someone* been telling you that I'm a stroppy teenager who thinks I know it all, how I have a lot to learn, how I'm unable to follow instructions, how I don't listen, how wilful I am, how I refuse to sweep the floor from left to right downhill as you're facing the back door because if the draft comes under the door it blows the hair all over the shop?'

'No,' said Mum, going a bit pink. 'No one's been telling me that. At all, as it happens.'

'Hmmm.' Like I really believed her.

'So *is* that why she fired you?'

'I said I don't want to talk about it!'

'I know,' said Mum, 'and I said that is *fine*, we don't have to talk about it. Let's not talk about it. Look – we're not talking about it! It's negative. Let's concentrate on the good stuff and where you'll go next.'

'I don't want to talk about that either.'

'Sadie, you have started a Level 1 Hairdressing course. That's one day out of school a week! We need to sort the apprenticeship or this year is a complete waste of time, not to mention you can't enter that competition unless –'

'I don't want to talk about it, Mum!'

'Well we have to think about it, even if we're not talking about it,' said Mum.

She cannot just let things lie, my Mum. She has to poke them and prod them.

'OK.'

'And we have to talk about it before Monday because Monday you have college.'

'I know.'

Of course I knew that Monday I had college. And by Monday, everyone would be getting their entry forms for the Thames Gateway Junior Apprentice Hairdresser (or Barber) of the Year Award filled out and signed. Everyone except me, because as of an hour ago I was no longer eligible to enter.

3

Acid Perm Lotion

The hairdresser (or barber) must complete the entry form before or on the required date stated.

Guideline 3: Thames Gateway Junior Apprentice Hairdresser (or Barber) of the Year Award

Monday morning and when I arrived at college I saw that Aimée Price was wearing green earrings that matched her green bag that matched her green-and-white spotty shoes that matched her green-tipped nails. No wonder people called her Claire's Accessories behind her back.

She was sitting on one of the barber chairs we have in the student salon and her feet were up on another, matching shoes and all. These chairs are from Taylor Belshaw's Nirvana range – expensive kit with funky patterned seats like I plan to have in my own salon eventually. You can bet that Aimée Price wouldn't have a clue about quality salon chairs, judging by the way she put her feet all over them. She was also boring the pants off Florence, our lecturer.

'Misty really reckons I'm in with a chance,' she was saying. 'She's getting the senior stylist to do extra work with me to like coach me up and everything for the competition.'

Yeah. Well, Aimée was going to need all the help she could get. I knew the salon she worked in. Cissor's Palace – Unisex Hairdresser was at the south end of Roman Road, and it was as cheesy as it sounded. All the fittings looked like they were from the 1980s or something, and not in a good, retro way, and 1985 was when the owner, the famous Misty, last changed her hairstyle, by the looks of things. The woman wears it up in a scrunchie, and I'm pretty sure she still demi-waves in there. If you ask me, for an apprenticeship, Cissor's Palace – Unisex Hairdresser really sucks the big one.

Florence wasn't quite so convinced either. 'Aimée, I think if you work on your timing you could be in with a shot for the competition,' she said. 'But you do need to speed things up a little bit.'

Aimée Price needed to speed things up more than a little bit – I mean snails took a dump faster than Claire's

Accessories cut hair. I was waiting to hear what else Florence had to say about Aimée's chances when she caught sight of me.

'Oh, Sadie, have you filled out *your* form yet?'

'Er . . . not yet,' I said.

I lied. Of course I had filled it in. Of course it was sitting on the table in the lounge, ready to be signed off at the bottom by Aunt Lilah, who was the owner of the registered salon where I was doing my apprenticeship. Where I *had been* doing my apprenticeship. Until she fired me.

'Well don't forget, will you?' Florence winked at me. 'They have to be in soon.'

I don't mind saying that our lecturer thinks I can cut hair. She may say that Aimée's in with a chance if she speeds up a little, but Florence reckons I've got 'real talent'. The previous week I'd come top for my colouring. Florence said she thought it was professional standard.

'You're a performer, Sadie, even under pressure – which makes you ideal for any sort of competition situation. I don't want you to miss out on a chance like this.'

That's why I wanted to enter. That's why I'd had my heart set on it, right up until Aunt Lilah struck on Saturday. But I didn't feel like I could tell Florence about what had happened in the salon. She might have said it was my fault – which sounded about right. And I didn't want her to guess for one minute that maybe I'd tripped myself up and tried something out that the customer didn't necessarily want.

'You need to be objective about your performance,' Florence was always telling us. 'It'll help you improve. You need to be able to stand back and say, "I did that well" or "I didn't do that as well – I need to work on that." That way you'll keep getting better. If you make the same mistakes over and over and clients complain, then the chances are you're just being arrogant.'

I thought back to Saturday. Mrs Nellist hadn't complained about her new style. I was convinced that she liked her hair how I did it. But maybe I shouldn't have done it at all. I should have gone and got Aunt Lilah away from those Kit Kats and handed her the customer. I should've carried on sweeping up and washing heads. If I had, then I'd still have my job and I'd be handing in my form for the competition, and I wouldn't have been worrying about what was going to happen next instead of concentrating on my class.

We spent the morning learning about contra-indications for perming and did porosity and elasticity tests on each other's hair. Aimée was my partner and she took this as a licence to yank strands out of my scalp. This was not only painful, it was also annoying, being that I'd spent about half an hour before college twisting my hair up into a perfect French pleat. All through last year I'd had this customised 'Hairstyle a Day' calendar that Aunt Lilah and Uncle Zé had given me for my fifteenth birthday. It was the most perfect present and I was gutted when it had finally run out on my sixteenth birthday. I secretly hoped they'd get me another one, but they got me vouchers instead because Aunt Lilah said I was 'too difficult to buy for these days'. Vouchers didn't tell you what hairstyle to wear every single day of the year and how to do it. Without that calendar I was on my own. I mean, I had to decide for myself. That morning I'd decided on a French pleat, and now Aimée Price was busy dismantling it.

'Wow, Sadie, you hair is so porous –' (*yank*) '– must

be all the chemicals you use. You really shouldn't perm it, you know.'

'But I'm not going to perm it, Aimée – we're just doing this for class, right? This is an E-X-E-R-C-I-S-E.'

I swear, sometimes I wondered why I was doing this class, instead of training to be a rocket scientist or a neurosurgeon. I'd got some decent exam results last year and my predicted grades for this year's batch were pretty good. But some of the girls who wound up doing hairdressing were dumber than a box of hair. Were they really dumb though? I mean who'd just lost their job? Them or me?

'D'you think I'm thick or something, Sadie?' said Aimée, like she'd read my mind.

'No?' I said, not even attempting to sound convincing.

'Because you act like you're all superior and I am actually an incredibly intelligent, motivated and sensitive person.'

'OK,' I said, although I felt the words 'frighteningly stupid, lazy and dumb' summed her up better.

'My nan brought me up, you know,' continued Aimée, like I was interested or something, 'and she would never do a thing for me. She always says, "*you want something, Aimée? Well, go get it. You can have anything you want in this world, but the catch is you have to work out how to get it yourself.*"'

'Oh,' I said.

The truth is that I wasn't interested in Aimée Price's damage. I mean we all have our own tragic childhoods to overcome, don't we?

'So now, specially because my Nan's getting old, so she can't help me,' Aimée said, 'every time I have a task to do I just say to myself, "You want it – you work out how to go get it, girl."'

And I'll bet she'll have that on a bumper sticker when she gets her first pink-with-matching-interior car, I thought.

'You girls finished up there?' interrupted Florence.

'Sadie's hair is really porous,' said Aimée, snapping back from Aimée-Price-Self-Motivator into hairdresser mode.

'Acid perm lotion for you then, Sadie, if you were ever thinking of getting your hair permed, which I wouldn't advise by the way. Alkaline for you, Aimée.'

'You want it – you work out how to go get it, girl,' Aimée repeated in case I hadn't heard.

Oh, purlease . . .

Usually I was 100 per cent absorbed in my college day – I mean, compared to school it was a dream come true. Nobody blanked me at college; there were no ex-best friends like Shonna Matthews, who'd made my life a living hell last year. I had no 'history'. I didn't have to hide out in the library or the music room, nobody called me 'donor girl' and nobody knew I had a nerdy cousin Billy who played guitar. At college the teachers talked to you like you were a grown up and so mostly you behaved like one. Mainly I liked the sense that I was moving onwards with my goal, that even though the steps were small they were all in the right direction.

But that Monday just didn't feel positive. That Monday all I could think about, all day and even on the bus home, was the wretched competition form on the lounge table that needed Aunt Lilah's paw-print. And all I passed on that bus journey home, in between the skanky fried chicken shops, were hair salons and barbers. I had never really noticed just how many there were. Headlines, Concept Hair, Cissor's Palace, Curl Up 'n' Dye, Trimmers – I must have passed at least twelve along Roman Road alone. How was it that somehow I'd wound up without a job? I had no excuse – there were millions of salons out there. I just had to find another apprenticeship. But the memory of being fired still felt too hard and too raw, and for now all I could do was to look on with envy at these other salons and the people who worked in them. Were they better than me? Were they cleverer? It felt like they must be because they had jobs and I didn't.

And then just as I got off the bus I saw Mrs Nellist. I knew it was her because her neat little head looked slightly rosy in a certain light.

'Hello, love,' she said vaguely, and then she really recognised me and her face lit up. 'You know I'm glad I run into you,' she said, 'I've had so many compliments about me hair. The family were over on Sunday and my granddaughter just couldn't get over it, and my son. They love the shape and the colour. You are clever, y'know. I was going to pop into the salon and tell you, but I don't have to now. Ta-ra!'

And with that she was off, her little pink head bobbing away down the road, leaving me nodding and shaking my own head with the huge irony of it all.

4

This Was Starting to Sound Good

The trainee hairdresser (or barber) should be open to suggestion and input from professionals, clients and their peers.

Guideline 4: Thames Gateway Junior Apprentice Hairdresser (or Barber) of the Year Award

An hour after I got home, when I was just settling down on the couch with a cup of tea and the laptop to distract myself from the anxiety of not having an apprenticeship, the buzzer went. I'd been about to log on to this site I used to chat on all the time when I was really lonely last year. It's www.girlswholikeboyswhoplayWoW.com and I found it when my cousin Billy was in Nerd Frenzy Mode and playing World of Warcraft the whole time. I used to chat to Groovechick2 on there – she always had something positive to say. Lately though she seemed to have disappeared. She never responded to my updates about how cool my boyf was or how great college was. Then again, I wasn't online so much these days, so I guess she'd found someone else to talk to.

But today I kind of felt like I needed her. It was definitely a Groovechick2 moment. I wanted to tell her about the whole firing thing. I wanted to say **Feel like world is imploding. Lost my job, lost my purpose** — something like that. Maybe some friends are just there for the hard times. Maybe they feel like you don't really need them when things are great.

The buzzer went again. I got up off the couch and picked up the handset. It was my cousin Billy. Even in my less than great mood I noticed he was using way too much wax on his tips at the moment. You could even see it on the itty bitty security screen we have on our intercom. I must tell him some time. It doesn't really do anything for him.

'D'you wanna come up?' I said.

'I'm with Tony and Enrico,' he said. 'Can you come down?'

Enrico is Tony's older brother. He's twenty and so totally fit that you almost faint when he looks at you. He works in PC World in the workshop or something, so he's always pretty cashed up. Recently he bought a nice car, which is where I found them when I made it down to the front entrance.

Tony was in the back seat and when he saw me he opened the car door and got out. I liked how he did it. In fact I like the way Tony does pretty much everything. I read in a magazine that after six months you stop liking the way your boyfriend does everything and you start hating it instead, but that hasn't happened to me. We'd just had our first anniversary and I still even liked the way he got out of a car.

'All right?' he said and kissed me. He has to bend down like three feet to reach because I'm such a squirt.

Did I mention that Tony Cruz kissing me always makes me want to laugh? We've been together a whole twelve months, but I still can't quite believe my luck – it's so mental it makes me giggle. Tony is seriously a hot guy and I keep wanting to ask him, 'What are you doing with me?' In my most insecure moments – and I have tons of those, believe me – I think he's picked me out for one of those horrible dares. Like, *Do you dare to ask out the weird short girl with the shaky hands?*

Sometimes I do ask Tony what he's doing with me,

and he goes, 'I'm waiting for a bus — what the hell kind of a question is that?' And his voice goes up at the end and he nods the Tony Cruz nod because he is just soooo positive about life.

I'm never so optimistic though and I have to ask, 'But why are you waiting for it with me?'

'Because I like you.'

'Why?'

'Because you have brown eyes and a cute little mouth and — I dunno, Sadie. You do good hair.'

Tony always kisses properly. He generally greets me with a snogfest, and this time in the car park was no exception. And as usual a member of at least one of our families was present: Enrico was peering at me in the wing mirror of his car. I could see him out the corner of my eye while Tony and I were kissing. I should have been used to it of course. At first it was just Uncle Zé, but lately I'd noticed that it was never ever just me and Tony; it was me, Tony and Billy or Enrico. Maybe it's just a coincidence because we are all mates, but anyhow Tony and I have got used to doing all of our making out in public, because if we ever walk into a private space someone else invariably walks into it two seconds later.

It's generally Uncle Zé holding an everyday household object, like a cast iron saucepan or an electric carving knife, in a threatening manner.

'In my country you would have a chaperone, *anak*,' says Uncle when I complain about it.

'Yes, *tito*, but we're not in your country,' I say.

'Yes, but I'm still your uncle!'

You can't argue with that. You could try, but the fact is immoveable even if it is completely irrelevant.

Tony stopped the snogfest and I finally focussed on the here and now.

'What's going on then?' I said in the general direction of Billy and Enrico when I got my breath back.

'We want to talk to you, if you and my brother have finished eating one another,' shouted Enrico, smiling at me through the car window so that my knees went weak and I felt completely disloyal to Tony for just a nano-second. But I mean really – just because you're on a diet doesn't mean you can't look at the menu, does it?

There is quite possibly nothing more thrilling than travelling in a car with your hot boyfriend, your cousin (who, thanks to a great haircut, no longer looks like a geek even if he is one and is using too much wax on his tips) and your boyfriend's brother (who is better looking than God) at the wheel. Enrico has great taste in music too and the sound was just pumping out of the car stereo, vibrating through our chests – heaping possibility on top of possibility. I mean, who knew what was about to happen? It felt like anything could.

We drove slowly down towards Mile End and then turned left on to Roman Road. People stared into the car when we got to the crossroads, like they wanted to be riding our train, reading our book. Tony's shoulder was resting against mine. I was so happy that I had a shoulder and that he had a shoulder and that they were resting against one another. Luckily the small gestures made me happy, instead of *HUGELY FRUSTRATED LIKE THERE IS A FURNACE SWEEPING THROUGH MY ENTIRE BODY*, which is how Tony described his experience of our relationship most of the time.

'Enrico's come up with an idea about the salon thing,' said my cousin Billy from the front passenger seat.

'What salon thing?' I felt my spine arch in irritation. 'Are you wanting me to go back and apologise to your mum or something – get my old job back?'

Enrico pulled up at the kerb. 'You can go beg Billy's

ma for your job back if you want, Sadie, but that wasn't what I was going to suggest.'

'OK . . . suggest away,' I said.

I was flattered that Enrico was taking any interest at all in my life, being that he was so good-looking and successful and everything. I decided he must really like his brother a lot.

'What d'you think of this place?' said Tony.

Opposite the car was a salon I knew only too well. CISSOR'S PALACE – UNISEX HAIRDRESSERS it said, in red block lettering on a shiny black background. In the window I could see Misty with that faithful scrunchie securing her hair à la 1985. Aimée Price was probably in there somewhere too, boring some customer stupid with her motivational slogans.

Go get it, girl.

So what? Was Tony suggesting I go and ask Misty for a job?

'You've gotta be kid–' I started.

'Not that one,' said Tony. 'This one.'

I hadn't noticed but we were parked bang outside an ultra-modern salon with tinted windows and coloured spotlights. It was called Stylee Stylee, Roman Road. For this area it was pretty fashionable. I'd never been in it – in fact I was fairly sure I'd never even heard of it or seen it before.

'Looks OK,' I said. 'What about it?'

'It's pretty new,' said Enrico, 'and it's run by an old friend of mine.'

'Oh?'

'Dariusz Zengelis,' said Enrico. 'I was at college with him. He opened this place about three months ago – had a chair in Soho somewhere before – and I hear he's looking for a Saturday person.'

Dariusz Zengelis was looking for a Saturday person. I, Sadie Nathanson, was looking for someone looking for a Saturday person. This was starting to sound good.

'Sounds good,' I said.

'We thought maybe you should apply,' said Billy helpfully.

'Sure, I should apply,' I said.

'Cool,' said Tony and he squeezed my hand.

'Go on then,' said Enrico, turning round and flicking his head towards the salon. 'What you waiting for?'

What was I waiting for?

I wasn't dressed for it. I didn't even have my

CV to hand. I needed to psyche myself up.

'I can't do it now,' I said. 'I'm not ready. I need to get my head together. I need my paperwork . . .'

'Well, get it all together, girl.' said Enrico, 'Saturday morning – go in there early and mention that you know me. It might just help.'

5

Another Great Moment in My Life – No, Really

In any job there is a surprise element, and hairdressing (or barbering) is no exception. The entrant should be able to demonstrate that they are well prepared for the unpredictable, surprising and exceptional.

Guideline 5: Thames Gateway Junior Apprentice Hairdresser (or Barber) of the Year Award

It was Friday night, and Friday nights in my family are traditionally spent at Aunt Lilah and Uncle Zé's place, with Mum and Billy of course, and my Great Aunty Rita, who travels down from Ilford on the number 25 bus. We eat a smorgasbord of Uncle's Filipino faves and my Great Aunty Rita's finest Jewish delicacies. Uncle's cuisine basically worships every part of a pig you can possibly eat and Great Aunty Rita has an absolute ban on pig products, being that she's kosher, but she likes to pickle everything in sight: cucumbers, cabbage, herring, beetroot . . . If you sit still long enough she'll pickle you. Of course, Great Aunty Rita is more my family than Uncle is – I mean she's blood – but somehow I haven't inherited the pickle gene so I tend to go for the pig-product end of the table. And both sides of the family fry everything that isn't a pickle. No wonder we never have guests.

Except that this evening we'd invited Abe. It was Mum's idea and it was a bad one in so many ways. Yet, strictly speaking, Abe is *my* family, so why shouldn't he come to Friday night dinner?

Great Aunty Rita simply cannot get her head around Abe. As far as she's concerned he's connected to our family by an unmentionable substance that she'd rather not have to think about, together with an act of extreme insanity that her niece Angela (that's my mum) committed some seventeen years ago when she decided to have a child on her own. To be fair to Great Aunty Rita, she has never had any problem with the product of what she considers to be this unholy and unnatural union, i.e. me. And I guess that this is something to be grateful for, but whenever Abe is mentioned she gets an odd look on her face. It's a look that says, *If anybody even mentions the words 'sperm donor' I may spontaneously combust*. So by and large we don't. I mean, why would we? Does Aunt Lilah continually mention the night that she and Uncle Zé conceived my cousin Billy? No, thank God, because otherwise we would all lose our dinners, pickles and all.

Great Aunty Rita has met Abe once before. On my sixteenth birthday this year we broke the habit of a lifetime and went out for a meal. Not at Aunty and Uncle's place. We went out in town. To a restaurant. Like normal people. But in the whole year we've known him, Abe has never been to Friday night dinner, so he's never had the full-on Family-From-Hell Nightmare Experience. I'd wanted to save him from it until the time felt right, because in the beginning I needed Abe to be separate from my actual family, somehow. I wanted Abe to be mine and nobody else's. Even Mum had done her best to stay out of things between me and Abe. A couple of times she'd stood chatting in the kitchen with Sarah for hours while Abe and I bonded. And we had walked Abe's Labrador Daisy together three times – just the two of us. We even worked on Abe's amazing garden one day. I was getting into the habit of being quite outdoorsy when I went to Bough Beeches.

My actual family are completely indoor people. And they are so loud, so dominating, so opinionated, that I sort of wanted to be sure that Abe and I knew each other at least a bit before letting my family loose on him. I mean, he might run away and never come back – and who could blame him really?

So anyway, there they all were when I walked in that evening: Mum, Great Aunty Rita, Uncle Zé, Aunt Lilah, Billy and Abe. I'd been home after school and got changed and then I'd decided to put a colour through my hair – partly because I wanted a new look for when I went into that cool-looking salon the next day to ask for a job, and partly because I hoped it would wind up Aunt Lilah. I had of course thought about boycotting Friday night dinner altogether, being that I was so pissed off at Aunty for firing me, and of course at the exact same time I was full of insecurity that she might have been right to do so. But I knew I was going to have to face her eventually and Mum had already invited Abe, and so I did Revenge Hair (a do that is sooo good your enemy will admit defeat) and used Goldfinger from SFX. I just put one streak in right at the front. It looked completely genius.

'We're all waiting for you – what happened to your hair?' said Aunt Lilah as I sashayed to the table like the room was a giant runway at the grand final of the Thames Gateway Junior Apprentice Hairdresser (or Barber) of the Year Award.

'It's totally natural,' I said, deadpan. 'I woke up and there it was.'

'Looks good,' said Abe.

I went over and gave him a hug and then gave Great Aunty Rita a hug too.

'How's my favourite great-niece?' said Great Aunty Rita – it's what she always says. I'm her only great-niece, but it does crack her up every time she says it.

'I'm good,' I said and sat down at the table.

Everyone tucked into the Friday night spread. I glanced over at Abe. He looked slightly bewildered by the offerings in front of him, but manfully piled his plate with pickled cabbage, pickled beetroot, *tsitsaron* (bits of pork), *gefilte* fish (fried fish balls), fried potato *latkes* (patties) and *lumpia* (fried spring rolls). I felt like offering him an indigestion tablet too. He'd suffer for it all later.

Conversation lurched around the table – if you could call it conversation. 'Conversation' implies that there is a talker and a listener. But nobody in my family is a listener and everybody is a gabber. Mum talked about her clients, who were suffering from something called 'the downturn in retail', Billy was sick of revising for his mocks, something had happened to Uncle Zé in the Cash and Carry, and Great Aunty Rita had been knocked out of this year's League of Ilford Jewish Women Spring Bridge Tournament. Aunt Lilah had something to contribute on just about every topic (surprise surprise). She is the original yakasaurus and loves nothing more than the sound of her own voice. She was thinking of getting a new floor put down in the bathroom.

'I'd like a stripe,' she said thoughtfully, 'with a sort of pink fleck. Like he had on that detective programme you were watching the other night, Zé.'

Uncle Zé said nothing.

'What was it called?'

'What?' said Uncle.

'That programme with the head in the bag. What was it called?'

'You mean *Blood Bath*?' said Uncle.

'Eughh,' said Mum. 'Could we talk about this after tea perhaps, sis?'

'No, but the flooring, Angela – it was lovely, wasn't it, Zé?'

'What?'

'The flooring on that programme. Y'know, the bit where they came in and the head was in the bag . . .'

'Lilah, I don't know what you're talking about, my love,' said Uncle. 'I wasn't looking at the flooring; I was looking at the head in the bag. How come you were looking at the flooring?'

'It sounds gross, Mum,' said Billy. 'Like *Serial Killer Interiors*.'

'Oh, all right then,' said Aunt Lilah. 'Just forget it.'

She looked crushed for a moment. Like her family didn't appreciate her sensitivity and attention to detail or something.

'How about you, Abe?' said Mum changing the subject. 'Did you have a good week?'

'Actually I had a letter from someone,' Abe said. He folded his serviette neatly in his lap and glanced up at me.

'Oh yes?' said Mum.

'Someone who I believe is my daughter,' said Abe. Then paused and corrected himself. 'Someone who I believe is *another* daughter.'

6

The Geek Gene

Excellent communication skills in hairdressing (or barbering) are vital to ensure good relations with colleagues and clients. The entrant must be able to show that they are a good communicator in order to be considered for the award.

Guideline 6: Thames Gateway Junior Apprentice Hairdresser (or Barber) of the Year Award

There was a sort of stunned silence, during which time my heart did a *tsukahara*-double-twist-with-crash-landing in my chest. In case you don't know, that's like a really complex vault that gymnasts do in the Olympics. But this wasn't gymnastics. This was a potential sister.

'What did he say?' boomed Great Aunty Rita after a few seconds. She's a bit deaf and her voice has a tendency to sound a bit like the foghorn on the Woolwich ferry.

Nobody responded. We all just sat there. I could

feel my face going very hot and I wondered if I was about to pass out. After all, I – Sadie Nathanson, only child – had just found out that I might have a sister. I gripped the table, trying not to swoon into my plate of mostly pig products. I am not joking. This sometimes happens to me.

'Well, my word,' said Mum eventually. 'That puts all our news to shame. This is huge.'

'It's big,' said Abe.

'What is?' said Great Aunty Rita.

'Abe might have another child, Rita,' said Aunt Lilah.

'Good grief,' said Aunty Rita, 'that was quick.'

Nobody knew quite what to do with that comment and so we all carried on like it hadn't happened.

'It turns out that this Marie – her name's Marie by the way,' continued Abe. 'Well, Marie's dad died last year and then she found out that he wasn't her natural father after all. Then her Mum got out all the papers with my details on it from the sperm donor website . . .'

I was quite sure that Great Aunty Rita flinched when Abe said the words 'sperm donor', but maybe her hearing aid was just giving her feedback.

'. . . and she's not so far away,' Abe continued,

oblivious to Aunty Rita. 'Canterbury, I think she said in her letter – I must have read it three times! But it's so hard to take in . . . even after Sadie getting in touch last year!'

'Well!' said Mum, and she reached under the table and squeezed my hand. I couldn't work out if this was meant to be a comforting gesture or if she was clinging on to me for support. She's like that, my mum. Over-emotional. Hysteria is my family's default position.

'Well, what d'you think about that, Sadie? Turns out you've got more family out there!' said Mum.

I could see tears behind her smiling eyes. *Please don't cry*, I thought. And then I looked at Aunt Lilah and thought, *Please don't say anything annoying.*

'Sadie – what do you think?' said Abe.

'Amazing,' I whispered, because it was truly amazing. 'Maybe I might get to meet her one day. Did she send a photo? I mean, do you know what she looks like?'

'No,' said Abe, 'it was just a letter.' I tried to picture a sister.

'Right now she doesn't know she has a half-sister. She's sixteen years old – exactly the same as you – and up until last week she thought her dad was her . . .

Dad.' Abe looked thoughtful for a moment. 'Odd what parents don't tell their kids, isn't it?'

It was odd. And, I realised, it was potentially sort of wonderful too . . .

On his way out later that evening, Abe said, 'I sent Marie my phone number – I'm hoping she'll call me.' He stooped so that his face was level with mine. 'Would you like me to mention you? It's up to you. I don't have to, if you're not ready for it . . .'

He put his hand on mine and I could see that both were shaking slightly. His hand; my hand. We were nervous. It was like we were both full of energy and it had nowhere to go.

'No . . . Yeah . . . Sure. Mention me to her. Tell her I exist. Give her my details if you like – she might want to call me or visit or something. I mean, we could get to know one another. I wonder what she looks like. I wonder what her hair's like . . .' And then I laughed because I knew I sounded ridiculous.

'You're a prize loon!' said Abe. 'If she calls I'll tell her you asked after her hair.'

Sometimes I just loved having a donor parent. You wouldn't get moments like this if you were conceived by a regular mum and a regular dad in a regular kind of set-up. You had other stuff of course – like maybe a dad who you got to know over loads of years and who you could look at pretty much every day of your life and know that you got your nose from him, or the way you lifted your eyebrows or your natural talent at fractions. But you didn't have moments where you finally found the provider of 50 per cent of your DNA spiral, or discovered a half-sister called Marie totally out of nowhere.

I knew I wouldn't be able to sleep that night. I went home and sat on my bed and stared into my embarrassing kiddy Snow White mirror for the longest time, imagining what Marie's face might be like, her eyes, her hair.

Of course, I always have to imagine the hair. I accuse my cousin Billy of being a guitar geek, or a computer nerd, but the sad fact is that I'm a hair geek. Really they need to put me and Billy in a lab and isolate that geek gene.

I don't even know if I can explain it, but hair to me is like this giant puzzle – like a labyrinth or something that you have to solve. You see it and you think, *Yuh-*

uh, I am going to figure out how this works. And then you get your fingers into it and sometimes it feels totally different from how you imagined it would feel, and it has this whole life of its own – like it knows what it's going to do – and sometimes it defies you with its curl or its porosity. But the thing is, you don't know how hair is going to work until you're in it and you don't know how you're going to be with the hair until you're doing it. And that pretty much sums up my life too.

I've been obsessed with hair forever – since I got my first Girls World Style Head, which was from Uncle's cousin Moss (the one who buys and sells on eBay for a living). The Style Head was a talking one from the Philippines and it said, 'Hello, *ang pangalan ko ay* Minnie!' when you switched it on.

I didn't really mind that the head spoke Tagalog, or that it was called Minnie, but what did matter to me was that it was blonde, which was a different colour to the redhead pictured on the box. And red was the colour I wanted. But instead of being devastated, I sneaked into Aunty's salon and did a red dye-job on the Styling Head. You know, I did pretty good for a six-year-old, even if I say so myself, and I've never looked back since. It's what made me the hair geek I am today. That and my DNA.

So now, when I was about to acquire a half-sister, I thought about Marie's hair and I wondered if it resembled my growing-out Cleopatra bob, or if it was like Abe's shaggy mess of curls that he had refused to let me loose on so far. (To be frank, Abe is a bit of a hippy. He could carry a buzz-cut. I think it would really improve his whole look.) Or maybe Marie wasn't like either of us — she might just be like the bits that connected us. There weren't many, granted. We had the shaky hand thing obviously, and we had similar round eyes, but people said that there was another subtle similarity too.

'There's something else about you and Abe that's the same,' Mum says. 'You don't look alike, but there's an expression, or it's how you hold yourselves. There's something that makes me know you're related.'

Would Marie have that something too?

7

Billy Being Weird Again

It is very important that the hairdresser (or barber) takes the time and trouble to talk to the clients. Lifelong friendships can be made in the hairdresser's chair and clients often look forward to chatting about their daily lives with somebody familiar whilst they are getting their hair done.

Guideline 7: Thames Gateway Junior Apprentice Hairdresser (or Barber) of the Year Award

Mum knocking on my bedroom door made me jump. She poked her head round and grinned at me with all her teeth showing, which she shouldn't really do because she's got this dead tooth at the front and you can see where it's a bit, y'know, grey. She'd just washed her hair and it was looking even more disastrous than ever before.

'Can I come in?' she said.

'Barbie's House is always always open . . .' I said, and I cheesed right back at her. (Yes, I still have the Barbie wallpaper and I am so over finding it embarrassing.)

'Are you OK?' she said, plumping herself down on my bed.

'Sure,' I said. 'Why wouldn't I be?'

I knew that she wanted to talk about Marie, but I felt as if she was my property, and I didn't want to discuss her with anyone who wasn't related to her. Which weirdly Mum wasn't.

'I just wondered how you felt about Abe's news, that's all. I mean, it was a pretty interesting piece of news.'

'Sure it was,' I said, 'and I feel OK about it.'

'Well, good,' said Mum, and she clasped my hand like she had at Aunty's last night when Abe had announced everything. 'I'm glad you feel OK. It must be very exciting for you.'

'It is,' I said, but I still didn't feel ready to share. 'I'm still, y'know, thinking about it.'

'Right,' said Mum softly, and she sat there for a bit longer, just smiling and clasping my hand and going, 'Right,' every so often.

I guess she was waiting for me to say something more

meaningful. But the thing was I didn't have anything else to say, partly because she was making such a big thing of it.

'All right, love,' she said eventually, 'I'll say goodnight then and see you in the morning.'

She kissed me and gave me a hug and then backed out of the room smiling, like she was a TV mom, minus the bleached teeth. I do love my mum and everything but I don't see how she manages to get it so wrong – she just does, *because* she's my mum.

After she closed the door my phone sprang into life. It was a text from Billy.

U ok? Abt your sista I mean – that is so coooool

Text wouldn't cut it. I called him right back.

'I'm a bit freaked,' I said. 'I can't stop thinking about it.'

'Me neither,' he said.

'Really? How come?'

'It's kind of weird,' said Billy, 'but I think we've been the same for so long now. It's just been us – "lonely onlys" and all that. I've always known that you understood what it was like and everything.'

'Billy, we were never "lonely onlys" – you've always been my brother.'

This was true. They put me in Billy's cot the day after I was born and he was one year old, and we'd been together in one situation or another ever since. Of course, we had nothing but our bonkers family and our geek tendencies in common. But we were still siblings.

'Yeah, but you're about to get yourself a real, live sister.'

'Half-sister.'

'Whateva – she's proper.'

'Well she's yours too,' I said, although this didn't feel quite right.

'Na,' said Billy. 'She's all yours and I think that's OK.'

'OK.'

'But I reserve the right to be jealous.'

'Really? You're jealous?'

'Sure.'

'Don't be jealous, Marie might be horrible.'

'Sadie, no one is horrible.'

Then there was a pause. It wasn't like a Mum-pause

though – it wasn't like he was smiling and clasping my hand, I mean, he was on the end of the phone. He wasn't even waiting for *me* to say something. It was more like he was waiting for *him* to say something.

He'd been doing this a lot lately when he called – always a lot of long pauses. He plays guitar in a band with my boyfriend Tony and sometimes I wondered how they got anything done at all – like rehearsing and writing and everything. What with Tony doing all that nodding and Billy doing all that pausing.

After a while I couldn't stand it any more.

'Billy?'

'Yeah.'

'Is something up?'

'How d'you mean?'

'I mean you keep going really, like, quiet on me or something.'

There was another long pause.

'Like that,' I said.

'Sadie . . .' said Billy.

'What?'

'D'you ever feel like everything's changing?'

'How d'you mean?'

'Like stuff is unsettling, like there's something going on.'

Pause.

'Like *what's* going on? I mean I know you're in sixth form and everything's starting to get serious for you, but it's not that big a deal, is it? I mean I'm doing GCSEs this year and I'm not exactly freaking out!'

Pause.

'Doesn't matter – I'll let you go to bed. See you later.'

And he was gone.

And it was weird.

I thought about Marie again when I turned off the bedroom light. You see, even though I wasn't so dumb as to think that Mum had been the only person who'd selected Abe's 'donation' off the website, I'd never even allowed myself to imagine that there might be more children out there – more children like me.

There was something so awesome about the thought of a sibling. I would never say this to Abe of course, but finding a sibling felt even more exciting than finding him, my donor dad. I couldn't put my finger on why, but maybe it was because there were so many possibilities with a sibling. A sibling could be your actual friend as well as your blood, your people, your kin, your DNA.

Lately I didn't score so well on the friend front, not since my former best friend Shonna Matthews axed me. I didn't miss Shonna, but I did miss the good things about having a best friend. Just the idea of Marie made me think about all that sharing you do with a girlfriend. I imagined us going shopping together, talking on the phone. Maybe she'd even let me do her hair.

As I drifted off to sleep, I realised I felt excited and oddly motivated. Now all I needed was a new Saturday job, and tomorrow I was going to go out and get one.

Chapter 8
Enrico Says Hi

The trainee hairdresser (or barber) should be prepared to approach local registered salons for Saturday placements. A direct approach, rather than by correspondence or email, is encouraged. Prospective employers will be able to judge interpersonal skills immediately and know whether you will be a good fit for their client base.

Guideline 8: Thames Gateway Junior Apprentice Hairdresser (or Barber) of the Year Award

Saturday, 8.30 a.m. Dariusz Zengelis did not smile once during our conversation at Stylee Stylee, Roman Road. He barely blinked even. He stared at me with his black pupils. It reminded me of my cousin Billy back in Juniors 4. Even now Billy never gets 'mildly interested' in a topic. He becomes consumed by whatever it is. In this case it was his *Bumper Book of Space* and it had this chapter about black holes and how they sucked you in and spaghettified you so that your legs and arms were stretched and you disappeared into nothing. And that's kind of what Dariusz Zengelis's pupils were like when you approached him: Black Holes of Doom. While I talked, he stared, and I felt myself being sucked in and disappearing into nothing.

'You have turned up on our busiest day of the week,' said Dariusz.

My eyes flicked round the salon, which looked empty and unbusy to me. But I didn't feel like contradicting him. 'I'm sorry about that – I just thought I'd hand in my CV and make an appointment for an interv–'

'How did you hear about the vacancy?' Dariusz interrupted, now flicking through his appointments book. His voice was bored and flat. His hair, which was long and dark with flecks of metallic grey, was slicked down close to his head, streamlining him. The man was a human Dalek.

'Oh, just on the grapevine,' I said. I didn't want to mention Enrico yet. I mean, I wanted to get the gig because I was good enough, not because I knew someone who knew someone. Enrico was my trump card.

Dariusz stared at me blankly. Perhaps I was coming

off too casual. So then I tried to sound keen.

'You see, I heard about your salon and I thought it looked kind of modern and interesting.' My voice echoed around the empty, silent shop. 'I thought I'd come in on the off-chance that you might give me a try-out. You see I want to enter this competition . . .'

STOP TALKING ABOUT THE COMPETITION OR YOU WILL BE EXTERMINATED! said Dariusz.

Well, that wasn't exactly what he said of course, but it might as well have been. That's what his eyes said anyway. His mouth remained shut.

'It's the Thames Gateway Junior Apprentice Hairdresser (or Barber) of the Year competition,' I continued. 'My lecturer says I stand a good chance because I have excellent technique and I can perform under pressure. I'm very enthusiastic, I'm good with people, I work really hard – but to qualify I *need* a job and a nomination.'

I was babbling now and I was also begging. It was the stony silence that did it. The total lack of reaction from my listener made me sound completely desperate. Which I was.

'I'll leave my CV if you like.' I held the envelope

67

containing my professionally prepared CV out to him. He took it reluctantly, like I'd handed him a chewed biscuit or an old sock. Then he stood up and moved towards the shop door.

YOU WILL LEAVE THE SALON NOW OR YOU WILL BE EXTERMINATED! said his eyes. I began to feel that the bottles of shampoo were chattier than Dariusz Zengelis.

And this was fine by me because I was ready to go. Except that I wasn't, because I needed the job. I needed the nomination.

I was desperate. As Dariusz was shoving me out the door, I said, 'Actually this place was recommended to me by a friend of yours – Enrico de Cruz. He says "Hi" by the way!' It was my last-ditch attempt to phoenix the situation.

There was a pause as we stood in the doorway.

And then, I can't be sure, because it did happen rather fast, but I believe that Dariusz Zengelis literally grabbed me by the scruff of my neck and pulled me back inside the shop.

'Who did you say?'

'E-E-Enrico,' I said. 'Enrico de Cruz.'

'You know Enrico?' said Dariusz, and his whole face

became animated and lit-up. The Dalek had gone and he actually sounded like a human being.

'Sure I know him,' I said. I mean, what was the big deal all of a sudden?

'But how do you know him? You're . . . how old?' He snatched up my CV from the counter and ripped open the envelope.

'I've just turned sixteen. GCSEs and all that. Big year.' There I was – babbling again. But now I wasn't the only one.

'OK, so you know Enrico because because because?' Dariusz snapped his fingers at me like it was the most important detail in the world.

'Because I know his brother – I mean, we like go out . . . he's my, er, boyfriend – well yeah, he is my . . .' I blushed. I always blush whenever I tell someone new about Tony. It's almost as if they can see him and they know how incredibly hot he is.

'Enrico's little brother,' said Dariusz half to himself. 'Enrico has a little brother . . .'

Really, the man was patronising.

'Tony's actually nearly seventeen,' I said. 'Anyway the point is that Enrico suggested I come in and speak

to you about the job because he said he knew you –
from college or somewhere.'

Now Dariusz's face was fixed into this grin and there
were lines at the corners of his mouth and his neck
looked kind of shrinkled. It was hard to imagine that he
and Enrico were mates. Dariusz looked way way older.
But at least his eyes were wide open and sparkling now
– no longer black pits of doom – and he was listening
to every single word I said. Really, when you compared
him to five minutes earlier, the transformation was
seriously weird.

'OK, OK. That's cool. That's completely cool,' he
said, and then he jumped up and skipped – yes, he
actually skipped – over to the water cooler and filled a
cup and drank it in one go. Then he ran his hands under
the spout and sprinkled water through his hair.

'Phew! It's hot in here!' he said.

It wasn't, but it *was* kind of oppressive.

'Well, Dariusz,' I said, 'you have my CV and it's
been good to meet you, so I'll just go . . .'

'Where you going?' he boomed at me.

'I was just going out the door . . . back to . . .

well, back to my life, I suppose. I told my mum I was going to nip down here and have a chat and leave my CV. I mean I knew you'd be busy, it being Saturday and all . . .'

'Well, you're in luck because I had two cancellations this morning and so my first appointment is ten o'clock,' said Dariusz. 'Then it's slog, slog, slog, slog, slog until our last customer. I won't be out of here until eight – earliest. But we need to try you out!' he said. 'We need to see what you can do. Come!'

He beckoned for me to follow him, and I obeyed, completely confused. I mean one minute the man was booting my backside out the door and the next he was practically holding me hostage.

'Bag and coat, please,' he commanded.

I obediently handed over my bag and coat. Dariusz hung them in the coat cupboard. Then, wordlessly, he presented me with a tabard. It was brown with white comic-book writing which said **Stylee Stylee** on the front and **Roman Road** on the back, and there were pockets for brushes and pins and scissors.

'Now come with me.' Dariusz frog-marched me to

a styling station and handed me a pair of shiny scissors. Then 'VENUS!' he yelled, so suddenly and so loudly that I nearly dropped them.

A very small woman wearing a housecoat and clutching a bright-pink feather duster appeared from the back of the shop.

'This is Venus,' Dariusz said to me. 'She cleans my salon and she will be your model. You have one hour.'

Huh? I wasn't entirely sure what I was being asked to do here. I mean, didn't Dariusz want to watch how I swept the floor? Florence had prepared us for these interviews and assured us that the most we'd be tested on would be a consultation and a hair wash.

'One hour?' I repeated.

'One hour before my first customer arrives and it gets completely manic around here. You can give Venus a whole new look if you like.'

A whole new look? I stared at Dariusz like he was the oncoming car and I was a rabbit.

'You want this job?' Dariusz stared back. The Black Holes of Doom had reappeared and were consuming me.

I nodded.

'My salon is the best there is around here,' said Dariusz, 'and I want the best staff. The best! And that includes my Saturday girl. Now show me what you can do . . .'

This was it. The test had begun.

9

The Transformation of Venus

The trainee hairdresser (or barber) should be able to
perform quickly and calmly under pressure. A typical salon
try-out will involve sweeping and washing, but the trainee's
creative and practical talents and the ability to work to a
tight deadline should also be tested.

Guideline 9: Thames Gateway Junior Apprentice Hairdresser
(or Barber) of the Year Award

Venus put down the feather duster and peered at me.

'You do khair?'

She spoke with a strong accent. When she said the
word 'hair' the sound came from the back of her throat,
like she was about to hawk right there on the shop floor.

I nodded. I have to admit that I wasn't really
concentrating on introductions here. I was only staring
at Venus's hair. It was lank and mousey brown and pulled
back with an elastic band.

I could sense that Dariusz was observing intently from the corner of the salon.

Oh God.

'Er, Venus,' I said. 'Come this way.' Now I was the human Dalek.

'Hold it right there,' said Dariusz before I could even guide Venus to her chair.

I stared at him. He stared right back. Eyes black. Unblinking. Then he spoke.

'OK . . . Sadie Nathanson,' he said, grabbing at my CV so he could read my name, 'you be the client.'

'Huh?'

'Go outside my shop, open the door . . .'

I did as I was told. Of course I did. I opened the door and went outsde, shutting it behind me. Then I opened it again and walked in being the client.

As I did so Dariusz appeared in front of me, making eye contact, smiling, holding himself tall and erect.

'Sadie, good morning!' he crooned. It was actually spooky – he was acting like he was really pleased to see me. 'Let me take your jacket and your bag.' He mimed these pointlessly. 'And what can we do for you today, my dear?'

We glided towards the chair and he seated me. Smoothly. Effortlessly. It was impressive actually.

'OK,' I said, 'I see. I need to make more eye contact. I need to slow it down . . . I need to . . .'

'Here's the thing,' said Dariusz, interrupting me. 'Think of a word. It needs to be a word that has an effect on how you speak, how you think and how you hold yourself. It needs to give you poise.'

I couldn't think of a word that would do that. What word would do that?

'My word,' said Dariusz, as if reading my thoughts, 'is "brush".'

He rolled the 'r' when he said it.

'Brrrrush.' He said again.

'Brrrrush.' I tried it. I rolled my 'rrr's.

'And again,' said Dariusz. 'Lift up your chest. Breathe deeply and "brrrrush".'

I did all of those things.

'I'll be the client,' said Dariusz and he went and stood outside the door of his own salon. I fully admit that there was a part of me that wanted to turn the key and run out the back all the way home to my bed and get under the duvet and never come out, but instead I stood in the wings of the salon like I was about to go on stage. As I heard the door open I whispered the word 'brrrrush', my chest rose and I glided to the door.

'Good morning, Dariusz,' I said with dignity, honour and grace. 'Would you like me to take your –'

'Not bad,' said Dariusz flatly, immediately deflating my balloon of poise. 'Now do Venus.'

I said 'brrrrush' to myself, welcomed Venus, guided her to the nearest chair and she sat down. We both stared at her reflection in the mirror.

I breathed deeply, watching my chest rise and fall and clearing my mind. It's this relaxation technique I copied off the school librarian, who is like the most weirdly laid-back person I've ever met. I combined this now with thinking 'brrrush' and it totally did the trick. I was a pro.

'What would you like me to do for you today?' I said brightly, trying to sound *'in control but not too bossy'* in the way Florence had tutored us.

'Well,' said Venus, 'usually I say nussing too fancy-schmanzy, but it's my son's birthday tonight so we can go glamour!' She opened her mouth wide and laughed, and I saw that she had only five teeth in the top row.

'Glamour' was going to be our challenge for the remaining fifty-nine minutes.

I grabbed a comb and quickly began to tease out her hair to see how it felt, how it worked. She'd clearly been styled by a hair-wrecker, but I'll admit that the dye-job wasn't bad. I mean, Venus must have been pushing sixty-five and there was no grey. I guessed that this was a legacy from another try-out trainee who didn't get the job. I wondered where they'd gone wrong. I wondered if they'd refused to say 'brush' or if they couldn't roll their 'r's.

After washing I combed through again, all the while feeling the hair and trying to channel the style that Venus didn't know that she'd always wanted through my hands. My hands were my tools. They were my secret weapons and I had to be in control of them at all times. *Glamour, glamour, glamour*, I thought as I ran them through the hair. In my head I flicked through my 'Hairstyle a Day – One Year of Original Styles' calendar. I thought of a 1970s Farrah Fawcett flip, I thought of 1980s big perms, and then I counted back to when Venus was young because it occurred to me that glamour was all about your particular era – about who you looked up to when you were in your teens. Glamour for Venus was at least fifty years ago: Sophia Loren, Audrey Hepburn, Elizabeth Taylor – glamorous 'dos with lift. Thank God for the calendar. I knew how to do that hair.

'If it's a party then let's make it really special. I'm going for a modern beehive,' I said. 'It's like a bouffant with tendrils. And we're not going to sweep too tightly so there's more height.'

'Sankyou, deary,' said Venus and she smiled at me.

I took my scissors, a comb and a deep breath.

Snip. Snip. I removed a centimetre all over.

I dried, divided and back-combed. I gathered, smoothed and secured into a ponytail. I flipped the pony forward and gripped it in a horseshoe band. I could feel Dariusz's eyes boring into me and I steadied my hands. I flipped the hair back over and took care to fold loosely to create more height. Then the secret ingredient; almost an entire canister of spray. Once the sides were secure I folded the remaining ends around my finger and used the tail comb. Finally I needed an accessory to insert in the back. I stared wildly around the room for inspiration. In a moment of pure genius I spied the bright-pink feather duster. I pulled out a single neon feather and blew off the dust before inserting it into the back of the 'do, where it sat proudly, gently wafting in the air.

Man on the mountain.

Mission accomplished.

Venus was delighted. I'm convinced that when she looked in the glass she saw Sophia, Audrey and Elizabeth looking right back at her.

'Ees beautiful. I like verrrry much.'

Dariusz didn't do delighted, but he gave me the job.

'I want you to start now. This minute. It's ten o'clock and we are back-to-back all day. I pay minimum wage and you get to keep your tips.'

'OK!' I said, clasping my hands together to stop the shaking.

I needed to text Mum. I wanted to tell Tony. I couldn't wait for Aunt Lilah to find out! But before I could do anything I looked up and there was Dariusz holding out a broom to me.

'I don't have trainees in my shop who won't sweep,' Dariusz continued.

'Oh.'

I really needed to text Mum. Just to let her know I wouldn't be back till late.

'We all sweep in here,' Dariusz said. 'I sweep. My other stylist Misha sweeps, and you especially sweep, and that's starting NOW!'

With that Dariusz Zengelis handed me the broom and I was off, sweeping the shop floor (in whichever direction I chose) in my new tabard and loving every minute of it.

10

Neighbours From Hell

Good relations with all visitors to the salon should be maintained, whether clients or local traders.

Guideline 10: Thames Gateway Junior Apprentice Hairdresser (or Barber) of the Year Award

It was only when I stood behind the sinks at Stylee Stylee to wash people's hair that I noticed the salon opposite. How unfortunate that of all the places in all the world it had to be Cissor's Palace – Unisex Hairdressers.

I had landed up working bang opposite Aimée Price. Even though I'd been concentrating practically 100 per cent on washing heads since Dariusz's first client, so that now my hands were totally wrinkled and my neck was stiff from bending over the sinks, I couldn't avoid catching glimpses of Miss Claire's Accessories over the road as her red jacket and matching headscarf and earrings bobbed about in the window. And once seen, she was impossible to ignore. Then she looked across and started waving. I looked behind me to where the other stylist Misha was stood. Misha wasn't looking at Aimée Price. She had her back to the window and was having an intense discussion with a client about whether or not to try a side-sweep. Personally I thought she should go for it.

I turned back to the sink and saw Aimée Price crossing the road and coming in the door.

'Yoo hoo! Knock knock,' she said to Dariusz, who was writing in the appointments book at the front desk.

'Good morning, young lady,' said Dariusz. 'How are we today?'

'Well, I'm fine,' said Aimée. 'I've just spotted my friend over here.' And she bustled through to the back of the shop.

I busied myself with washing the sinks out, removing the hair from the plugholes, saying the word 'brrrush', anything but to look up and see her – but here she was. I checked over my shoulder again, but Aimée really did mean me.

'Hi, Sadie,' she said.

She was smiling at me, urging me to play the game. I found I had no choice.

'Hey,' I said. 'It seems like we're neighbours.'

'You're gonna have to put up with me coming in and out of here all day long,' giggled Aimée.

'Oh? Why's that then?'

'Because I've got my eye on your boss is why,' she whispered loudly.

No wonder she was being so friendly all of a sudden.

I wanted to say, 'You go get it girl. In fact, you can have it.' But what I actually said was, 'You like Dariusz?' trying hard not to sound like her taste in men stank. He may have employed me, but the guy sure was weird. I hadn't forgotten his behaviour earlier in the day.

Dariusz Zengelis had like a split personality or something. He seemed to be fine with everyone else, but even when he was trying to be nice to me, he still had difficulty moving his mouth into something that resembled a smile. I'll admit that he could cut hair – from the first client I could see that he was some kind of hairdressing virtuoso – and I planned to make the most of what I could from him. He let me observe him or Misha during the occasional quiet moments, encouraging me to move around the salon when I wasn't washing heads or sweeping hair. But how could anyone fancy a man whose eyes were like these black pits of doom? It was beyond me.

'Yeah, sure I like Dariusz,' said Aimée, giggling again. 'And now you're working here I have the perfect excuse to keep popping by.'

'OK,' I said. 'Whatever makes you happy.'

'In fact,' said Aimée, 'I'll pop by again later and we can go for a coffee. There's a nice place over the road we could go – if the boss gives you TEN MINUTES OFF!' she shouted the last bit.

'Sure I give my staff breaks,' said Dariusz, winking at me – which was like being winked at by a Terminator unit. It was just unsettling. I tried to smile back. And with that Aimée was gone, breezing through the shop and back over the road to Misty, the scrunchie and her world of demi-waves, mullets and punters who wanted to look like Jane Fonda or Boy George or other throwbacks my Mum used to watch on *Top of the Pops*.

I spent the rest of the morning helping Dariusz to put in low-lights, using the foil method of course. (Not like Aunt Lilah, who still tortures her clients with a streaking cap.)

'The most important thing,' said Dariusz, 'is the

neatness. You must be in control of your foils.'

I watched his lightning hands tearing the foil like he'd used a ruler and a spirit level.

'Now you,' he said.

I did one.

'Again,' he said.

I did another.

'Again.'

And on and on tearing and folding, and then applying the colour and folding again, but beautifully, like it was an art class not a dye-job. I started to think of the client like a sculpture and had to remind myself to say 'brrrrush' in my head before I spoke to her.

Eventually Dariusz squeezed out a compliment. Of course he wasn't over the top.

'Good job, Sadie,' he said quietly as I glided over to the comfy chairs, gently manoeuvring the client towards the lights and the copies of *Hello*.

At bang-on one o'clock Aimée came whizzing into the shop again, like a heat-seeking missile in matching accessories, and practically dragged me out of the place by my hair.

'Ten minutes?' I mouthed to Dariusz.

'Spoil yourself,' he said. 'Take fifteen.'

In the event I took twelve and a half. Aimée seemed to have so much to say.

'So I'd been working at Misty's for weeks – did I tell you she reckons I'm in with a chance at the competition?'

I nodded. And she continued.

'And then one day I was looking out the window and there was Dariusz . . .'

She pronounced his name with a 'j' sound at the end – like '*je t'aime*'. It was so pretentious.

'And we've been friendly ever since, but just lately I noticed that he's always around when I come in and he always makes an effort to make me stay and stuff. And I really think he might just be interested in me.'

I gave her a bit of a look then. Of course he was always around. It was his salon.

'He's quite old,' I said, and then I felt as if that sounded really bitchy seeing as we were *being friends* now, so then I corrected myself. 'Mature, I mean. Which can be a good thing, can't it? Boys our age can be such a drag.'

I thought of Tony and the way that he sometimes

leaned his head over and closed his eyes so that he looked really deep and intense, and the way he sang when he was on stage with Billy's band, again with his eyes closed. And I felt bad for what I'd just said as he didn't seem to be the least bit of a drag. Not at all.

'Oh God, *yeuchh*!' said Aimée. 'Boys our age are just a nightmare. I mean, I know you're going out with . . . whatsisname . . .'

'Tony.'

Aimée knew full well that I went out with Tony. She didn't go to my school – she went to the Catholic one around the corner – but she still knew more people there than I did and she certainly knew all the gossip.

'Tony Cruz – that's right – the one with the hot brother!' said Aimée.

I was instantly irritated. I don't know why. It wasn't like I was the only one to notice how fantastically buff Enrico was.

'I guess Tony's mature for his age then?' said Aimée. 'But you know most of them are just pathetic juvie kids, right? I mean, did you hear about Alvi Tucker and Shonna Matthews?'

Even I'd heard that story (and I'm so short that

nothing reaches me!). Alvi Tucker had snogged Shonna Matthews (my ex-best friend) at a party two weeks before. Within days some graffiti had appeared in the boys' toilets, claiming 'Shonna Matthews Has a Tongue like an Ox'. Tony and Billy had laughed like drains when they told me, and I must admit I thought it was pretty funny. I didn't care much for Shonna, but I had a sneaking suspicion that she probably could have written the same thing about Alvi if she'd really wanted to. But why *would* she have wanted to? What would have been the point? Why humiliate some other human being so pointlessly?

Aimée was right. Most boys our own age were unhip, juvie losers. They were insecure and immature. I'd just got lucky with Tony

I zoned back in to hear, 'Anyway, Dariusz is only twenty-nine.'

'Twenty-nine?' I shrieked, because twenty-nine sounded so ancient. How could Aimée fancy a twenty-nine-year-old? Then I tried to cover it up and I said, 'I thought he was a lot younger – I mean he and Enrico were mates at college and Enrico's only twenty.'

'No, he's definitely twenty-nine,' said Aimée,

'because he said his next birthday would be the big three-oh. He went back to college to do some business courses a couple of years ago. You know, for his "professional development". He's been hairdressing for years. We talk, y'know . . .'

Then Aimée proceeded to give me another one of her lengthy trainwreck biopic moments, complete with motivational slogan – this time involving her nan's dog, who had something wrong with its back legs. ('He wanted something; he got it – even with two legs.') I zoned out again.

'D'you want another coffee?' said Aimée.

'Better not,' I said. 'I need to get back – I have to make a good impression on Dariusz. It's my first day.'

It was only when these words were out of my mouth that I realised what I'd said and, without missing a beat, Aimée came right back at me.

'If you don't mind my asking,' she said, 'weren't you working in a different salon before? I mean, I was a bit surprised to see you at Stylee Stylee. Isn't it a bit late to be starting somewhere new?'

Aimée Price was digging. She was hoping against all hope that I might be about to flunk out of the competition and leave the field open for her.

'I guess I fancied a change,' I said as casually as I could. 'Dariusz's salon interested me. It's different from all the others around here. He had a chair in Soho before and everyone says he's really talented. I wanted to learn from someone really good.'

I was convincing myself even. In this new version of events I had left Aunt Lilah's salon with the express purpose of scoring this job. I was the success and Aimée, who was still working at Cissor's Palace, was the failure.

'Well, I just hope he signs the competition form for you, Sadie,' said Aimée and she raised her eyebrows meaningfully – like she knew something.

'W-W-Why wouldn't he?'

She shrugged. 'Just that when I was chatting to him the other week he said he hated hairdressing competitions – didn't believe in them – thought they should be banned.'

My stomach lurched. My new boss hated competitions? My new boss thought they should be banned? If that was true, where did that leave me?

Aimée Price was smiling at me as I left the coffee shop. I noticed that she had a large smear of red lipstick on her tooth that was the exact same shade as her red jacket and her red earrings and her red headscarf. I could have told her about it.

But I decided not to.

11

Five Foot in Heels

Clear communication with the client about what you're doing and why you're doing it is very important. This way there can be no misunderstandings.

Guideline 11: Thames Gateway Junior Apprentice Hairdresser (or Barber) of the Year Award

At seven o'clock Dariusz said I could go home. He emptied the contents of the plastic cup he kept at the counter with my tips in it into my palm.

'You done good, girl,' he said. 'It's your first day, and it's a good first impression.'

I made my way to the coat cupboard feeling six foot tall, which for someone who only achieves five foot in heels means that I was buoyed up by an awful lot of good vibes. I passed Misha, who was still surrounded by clients. She mainly did black hair and she was in the middle of sectioning for a complicated fusion weave. I knew you had to get your partings really clean for fusion and Misha was slicing through this client's hair using her comb like a knife. I stopped to watch for a moment.

I could feel Dariusz watching me watching Misha.

'See what she's doing there, Sadie Nathanson?' he said. 'Now you try.'

Misha smiled and winked at the client, and then handed me the comb.

I tugged the hair down to get the parting. Some of the hair came and some of it didn't. The parting looked messy. I tried again, tugging slightly harder. The hair frizzed up.

'Hard,' said Dariusz.

'Don't be scared,' said Misha. 'Hard doesn't hurt.'

So I pulled hard. I sliced with precision. The part came clean and the hair lay flat. The client didn't break either.

'Good,' said Dariusz. 'And again.'

I did it again. And again. And fifty times more I sectioned hard and fast for that fusion weave until Dariusz told me to stop.

'You are fortunate to get this gig, let me tell you, honey,' said Misha. 'Dariusz is the best around here. I don't know what you have that is so special, but this is a lucky break for you.'

I didn't know what I had either. I had Enrico as a contact and that had got me through the door in the first place. I hoped that it wasn't what had secured me the actual job. I thought of Florence telling me I had real talent, and I thought of the pink feather in Venus's hair.

'You show yourself here again next Saturday,' said Dariusz, opening the door to the shop for me. 'Same time. You work like that every week and we'll get on fine. Just fine.'

'Thanks, Dariusz,' I said. 'For the job and everything, and will you sign my form for me next week?'

I just blurted it out. I had to see if Aimée was right.

'Form?'

'It's the Thames Gateway Junior Apprentice Hairdresser (or Barber) of the Year Award. It's like this big competition and they hold it in this arena place and you have to cut and colour and, y'know, regular stuff, but you have to be nominated by your salon.'

'Sure, sure – we'll see how we go.'

This wasn't really the answer I wanted, but it wasn't

an outright 'no' either. And he hadn't said anything about hating competitions. He just sounded like he didn't care one way or the other. I would have to be patient and pick my moment next time.

'You tell my friend Enrico to stop by here some time,' said Dariusz. 'I haven't seen him in the longest time.'

It was weird but his face sort of softened when he said that. His iron jaw went slack. But maybe I imagined it.

'Bye, Dariusz,' I said.

I'd put in a ten-hour day at Stylee Stylee, and even though my back ached from sweeping and leaning at the sinks and repeating every move fifty times and saying 'brrrrush', the day had flown like it had always failed to at Aunt Lilah's.

Aunt Lilah . . . Mum . . . Eeeek! I'd forgotten to text anyone in all the excitement and busyness of a new job.

I checked my phone and sure enough it showed five missed calls. Three were from Mum, but two were from Tony I was pleased to see. He'd sent me two texts as well.

But I had to deal with the difficult thing first. I called Mum.

'I'm on my way back from that salon I told you about. You'll never guess what . . . I scored a job there!'

'That's great, love,' said Mum uncertainly. Then I heard Aunt Lilah in the background going, 'Is it her? Is she safe?' in one of her famous stage whispers.

'Can you do me a favour, Sadie love?' said Mum.

'Sure.' I knew exactly where this was leading.

'Next time you go out in the morning and tell me you'll be coming back soon and then you stay out for ten hours – well can you just ring me to let me know what the hell –' She checked herself. 'What you're doing for the rest of the day.'

I could hear her trying to keep the anger out of her voice, but I couldn't keep it out of mine because she'd just burst my bubble.

'I got a job!' I yelled. 'Why d'you have to pee on my parade every single time?'

'Because it's *my* job,' Mum yelled back. 'I AM PAID BY THE GOVERNMENT TO RUIN EVERYTHING GOOD THAT EVER HAPPENS TO YOU!'

'Yeah, well that's how it feels.'

'Look,' said Mum, all calm again, 'just call me next time, huh? Or text me. You are so lucky I don't get in too much of a panic these days when I don't know where you are.'

Oh God. Not *much* of a panic? Who knew what that actually meant? Perhaps she'd only called two out of three emergency services this time, as well as making Uncle Zé call the hospitals and drain the canal.

I wandered back down Roman Road scrolling through the texts from Tony (**Miss u 2day babe** and **Where is u?**) and then a message popped up from Billy.

Cn u call me?

Billy – wanting something as usual, but not saying what. Weird and mysterious again. Well, he would just have to wait.

12

Scissors and Sisters

The trainee hairdresser (or barber) must describe in a personal statement why they wish to enter this competition.
Guideline 12: Thames Gateway Junior Apprentice Hairdresser (or Barber) of the Year Award

'The wanderer returns!' Aunt Lilah called out when I walked through the door of our flat.

I mean, I had barely made it over the threshold and the woman was already on one. Where to go? Where to hide? I wondered if I could make it to my bedroom without having to encounter Aunt Lilah, Uncle and whoever else was hanging out in the lounge winding Mum up into a frenzy.

Then I decided on a long-stay shower and diverted towards the bathroom. If I spent an hour in there hopefully everyone would get bored and go home. My fingertips were on the door handle, but I didn't quite make it.

'Sadie, love!'

And then there was Mum at the lounge door, all forced smiles and grey tooth. It was too late. Time for the interrogation.

'Hi!' I said and hugged her. In a split second I decided that upbeat was my best chance to change the mood from inquisition to congratulation. 'You're looking at the brand new apprentice for Stylee Stylee, Roman Road! How cool is that?'

Mum looked a bit baffled. I'm guessing she'd been bracing herself for a sulk and a stomp. I'm guessing Aunt Lilah had been fuelling that fire. But sometimes I was actually able to stop myself delivering what was expected – and this time I'd even surprised myself.

'That's just great, love!' said Mum. 'But please next time –'

'Let you know where I am,' I interrupted. 'I know and I'm sorry. I just got completely caught up. It's such a cool salon and Dariusz is all *bam! bam! bam!* with fifty gazillion clients and I was . . .'

'Busy place, is it?' Aunt Lilah and Uncle Zé were behind Mum now. Both of them had the same facial expression; eyebrows raised, expectant. Aunty's hair was in this chic chignon knotted at the neck. It looked cute actually and distracted me from the fact that she was challenging me to say that Stylee Stylee made her salon look like one of those towns in old films that Uncle likes watching, where they're so deserted that there's actual tumbleweed blowing down the middle of them. Tumbleweed which presumably I would be made to sweep up from left to right as you're facing the back door.

I wasn't going to be drawn in though. I kept my eyes on the chignon and I said, 'It's pretty busy – I love your hair, Aunty. How did you get it to DO that?'

That was enough. Aunt Lilah and I were doing chignons for the next forty minutes. Even though I'd been on my feet all day, up to my elbows in hair, I just couldn't get enough of it. We re-did Aunty's, then we did mine – which took ages because I'm growing out my Cleopatra look and it's all a bit 'endy', so hard to make it neat. Then we threatened to do Uncle's – that got rid of him. ('When you girls start on the hair it's my signal to leave.') And finally I started on Mum's, and Aunt Lilah left me to it. Mum's hair involved giving her a trim and obliterating for good those two hairstyles she's always trying to find her way back to.

I was just blow-drying to perfection when the phone rang. It was Abe.

'She rang late Friday night,' he said. 'Marie rang me. I mean, I've spoken to her.'

Woah. That caught me out. In today's excitement I'd totally forgotten about my new half-sister. And now he'd actually spoken to her.

'You there, Sadie?' said Abe. 'Did you hear me?'

'Yeah! Yeah!' I said. 'I just can't really believe it. I can't really take it in. It's too huge. Did you tell her about me? Does she know I exist?'

'That's partly why I'm calling you,' said Abe.

'Oh.'

'You said I could pass on your details.'

'Yuh. Definitely.'

'Well, I did,' said Abe. 'I passed them on and she said she'd call you or email you or something.'

'Wow.'

'I hope that's OK, I mean you did say I should. I gave her your address and everything. I think it would really help her to talk to you – or write to you. She seems *really* nice. Super nice.'

'Is she definitely gonna contact me – I mean when did you pass this on?'

'Friday, on my way home from dinner. She wanted to know all about you. She wanted to know what you looked like – what you did. Everything. She was a lot more interested in you than she was in me.' He laughed. 'I was a bit miffed actually.'

'So what did you tell her?'

Abe paused. And then he said, 'I told her you were funny and fashionable and creative, and that you had a loud, interfering family who drove you crazy. I said you were a hairdressing nut and pretty good at it and that you wondered what her hair was like.'

'Oh God – you told her that?'

'It was fine!' said Abe, 'It made her laugh – a lot.'

When I put the phone down I started doing this thing that I haven't done in the longest time, where I start looking at my life through someone else's eyes. I used to do it through my dad's eyes – I mean, before I knew that my dad was Abe. Now I was doing it through my sister's eyes – through Marie's eyes. Like there was a camera over my shoulder with me doing the commentary. Like, *Welcome to the wonderful world of Sadie Nathanson. This is*

*my family — aren't they incredibly annoying? See what I have
to put up with?*

13

Weird Chemistry

The trainee hairdresser (or barber) should be prepared to put in extra hours if they wish to be endorsed to enter the competition by their registered salon.

Guideline 13: Thames Gateway Junior Apprentice Hairdresser (or Barber) of the Year Award

I carried on doing the camera-over-the-shoulder thing at college on the following Monday during the sectioning practical. *I'm a trainee hairdresser, these are the other students on my course. Aren't they a bunch of lamers?*

'OK, class, gather round,' said Florence. 'Sadie's sectioning is razor-sharp. Now show them,' she said to me like I was her performing monkey, which I kind of was but didn't mind.

I breathed deeply and in my head I said the word 'brrrrrush'. I had poise. I had dignity.

I did a section and then another section; the steel

comb came down hard through the knots and tangles of the dummy's hair, and then quick as a flash I twisted the section into the butterfly clip, super-fast and neat, just like I'd seen Misha do on Saturday evening; just like Dariusz had made me do until I thought my arms were about to fall off. To me this method made complete sense. If you pulled fast and hard then it didn't resist nearly as much as if you tugged slowly and carefully – like pulling off a plaster.

'I'd say you've been practising,' said Florence.

Misha. Dariusz. This was down to my new job. All of a sudden it felt like being fired by Aunt Lilah was the best thing that had ever happened to me – although there was still a chink of 'don't get cocky' keeping me in check.

'I guess I have,' I said.

'And I hope you have your form for the competition?'

'Damn. Forgot it again!' I said.

I had not forgotten it. It was still on the lounge table, all ready and waiting for Dariusz's signature. There was no question that he just had to do it this coming Saturday, otherwise I'd miss my chance to enter the competition altogether. It needed to be received by the Thames Gateway Junior Apprentice Hairdresser (or Barber) of the Year Award panel by next Wednesday, which meant I would have to send it next Monday latest to ensure it got there on time.

'Well, I have your reports prepared, sealed and signed, girls,' said Florence to the us. 'So you can include them with your entry forms.'

It was Florence's report plus our own personal statements that would narrow down the field to the two hundred contestants on the day, and then we'd be narrowed down even further in the morning heats until there were just twenty finalists for the afternoon.

My personal statement, which needed a final tweak, went something like this:

I feel I'm ready to enter this competition because my tutor has told me that I perform well under pressure. I have been cutting and styling hair for friends and family for at least two years, and have worked part-time in a registered salon for almost three months, washing and trimming and, more recently, colour-treating hair.

(Here I neglected to mention that I'd been fired from

that salon and had only been working at my current salon for one week.)

> *I began my Level 1 Course in Hairdressing in September and have been told that my work is promising and professional. I am passionate about the creative, practical and commercial aspects of hairdressing and think I can bring my own vision to this field.*

I felt like the statement still needed work. Aimée reckoned we needed to use the word 'passionate' otherwise we wouldn't even make the heats. Apparently that's what Misty had said. I wasn't comfortable with it though. It sounded phoney. Perhaps it was better to be truthful. If I was going to be truthful then I would need to say something like:

> *I am obsessed with hairdressing. The first thing that occurs to me when I see anyone is, 'What is their hair doing? How does it work? Can I improve it?' This even applies to people on the telly: the Queen, the Prime Minister, the Pope. Nobody is safe.*

The trouble was I needed to find a way of telling the truth without sounding too insane.

On my way out of college Florence called me over.

'Y'know, Sadie, I'm a bit mystified as to why you're leaving it to the last minute for this competition. Anyone that can work like you just did this afternoon will be leading the heats.'

'Sure,' I said. 'I need to get the signature. I guess I keep forgetting.'

Why couldn't I just tell her the truth? Tell her I'd been fired and had to wait until my new, incredibly unpredictable boss who hated competitions felt like it was the right moment to sign the wretched form? Truth was, even I didn't know.

Aimée Price was waiting for me outside. She was all in black today, although her eyeshadow was picking out the purple paisley pattern on her handbag. You had to admire the attention to detail.

'No luck with Dariusz signing your form then.' She could barely conceal a smile.

'It's not a problem,' I said. 'I forgot to take it with me on Saturday, but I'm going to swing by the salon now.'

And there and then I decided. I just had to sort it – I

had to pick the form up from the lounge table and then stop in at Stylee Stylee and get Dariusz to sign it that instant . . .

The salon was shut, as I knew it would be. Most salons are closed on a Monday – Aunt Lilah's is an exception to this rule. But I guessed that Dariusz might be around doing the paperwork and that this could be the perfect moment to browbeat him into signing my form. No customer distractions. I could see a light on in the back office so I knocked on the window and sure enough Dariusz appeared, holding a product catalogue. He did not look so thrilled to see me, although he did open the door and allow me inside the shop.

'It's Monday,' said Dariusz leading me through to the back office. 'Why you here and it's Monday?'

He'd gone all Dalek again, when I first turned up on Saturday. And he was staring at me with those pits of doom. I really hated those pits of doom. It wasn't the warmest welcome.

'Well, I was just passing and . . .'

'Plus we're not really open on a Monday are we, Sadie? Or perhaps you didn't know this.'

Dariusz sat down and stared at his computer screen, writing things down on a product order. Why did he have to write things down? It occurred to me that he could have had an electronic database that would more or less order the products for him. The guy might be a genius at cutting hair, but he was clearly a dumbass when it came to technology. Billy would customise a database for him in like two Geeksville seconds.

'You know, I could do that electronically for you,' I offered, helpfully.

'Ah – and this is what you came all the way over here to tell me, is it?' said Dariusz. He'd done Dalek. Now he was doing sarcastic.

I took a deep breath. It was now or never.

'I actually came all the way over here on a Monday hoping you'd be here even though you're closed and all because I need you to sign my competition form. My tutor is getting really tetchy about it – she wants me to enter.'

It wasn't just my tutor. *I* really wanted to enter the competition.

I took the form out of my bag and waved it at him so that it made a flapping noise. Dariusz didn't even look up. He carried on transcribing the products on to his list.

Eventually he put down his pen and said, 'Sadie, life is not about winning competitions.'

'I know,' I said. 'It's just that . . .'

'No. I think you don't know,' said Dariusz, 'It means a lot to you this competition.'

'Well, yes, I suppose it does.'

'So, you turn up on Saturday and you work hard and maybe I will sign that form.'

'Thanks,' I said, not feeling the least bit thankful. I mean, why Saturday? Why not now?

'But until then you have to think,' continued Dariusz. 'Think about what will happen if I don't sign.' He stood up and went to one of the cupboards in the salon and opened it, searching for some product or another. 'I mean, will it be the end of your life if I don't sign?'

Yes was the short answer to that question. But I said nothing. I just smiled and nodded and left the shop.

Yes yes yes was what I thought as I stormed back along Roman Road. If Dariusz didn't sign my form on Saturday it *would* be the end of my life. I could see myself in twenty years' time featuring in a documentary about weird people who make a living buying and selling things on eBay, like Uncle Zé's cousin Moss does. They'd interview me and I'd go, 'I nearly made it as a hairdresser once, but Dariusz Zengelis refused to sign my form for the Thames Gateway Junior Apprentice Hairdresser (or Barber) of the Year Award.'

Well he was not going to ruin my life, I decided. He simply *had* to sign my form. And he was going to sign it on Saturday if it killed me.

14

French Plaits Look Cool

Working as an apprentice hairdresser (or barber) can occasionally be a frustrating experience. Trainees can be keen to try new techniques where salon owners would prefer them to master the basics. Patience should be practised by the apprentice, but putting oneself forward to observe and try new techniques where appropriate will be noticed and valued by your employer.

Guideline 14: Thames Gateway Junior Apprentice Hairdresser (or Barber) of the Year Award

There were two texts on my phone. One was from Billy.

Cn u call me?

Is it possible for texts to sigh? I swear the ones from Billy could. I hadn't called him back after Saturday's text because I couldn't bear the idea of more enigmatic silences. But I knew that I needed to. Don't get me wrong, I do love my cousin, but this antsy-pantsy phase he's going through makes speaking to him felt like a bit of an effort. But maybe I needed to make that effort.

The other text was from Tony. It made me smile. He still liked me. Even after a year, sometimes I just needed those texts to reassure me that Tony was still my boyfriend – that he still wanted to hang out with me. It didn't really matter what the texts said. It was just the fact of seeing his name come up on my phone. This one said:

Gig. Saturday. Cn u stylee stylee us? xxx

I smiled again. Why of course I could stylee stylee the band (even though Rock Dove would remain a lame name no matter how good they looked). Subject to pay and conditions. An image of the 50p lady was at the forefront of my mind when negotiating a deal.

Wot's the £?

While I waited for Tony's best offer, I paused at the

corner of my street and called Billy. I heard him sigh down the phone as he picked up.

'Hoozit?'

He sounded like he'd been asleep.

'Sadie!' I yelled. 'Read your caller ID! I'm your cousin.'

I wasn't looking where I was going, and I nearly collided with someone coming the other way along my street.

'Sorry,' I murmured.

As I glanced up to get out of the way I saw that it was a girl with a blonde French plait. I hadn't done a French plait since Juniors 4, when Shonna Matthews and I started a whole new trend that swept the entire school. The girl turned around and caught my eye and smiled at me like she knew me, which she didn't – or at least, I didn't recognise her. I did think how cool her French plait looked though.

'What's that?' said Billy.

'Nothing. I'm just proving the Don't Walk and Dial theory. Now, tell me what's going on?'

'Nothing really,' said Billy, and then he sighed.

Oh brother.

'Well you've texted me twice asking me to call . . . Is it about the gig?'

Pause. 'Well sort of . . . partly . . .'

'I've got some fantastic ideas for hair and stuff,' I squeaked, because truly I did. A whole portfolio of images had flashed through my mind when I read Tony's text. 'I could come over and talk you through them, or we could talk about it at school this week.'

Pause.

'Or not . . . Billy?' I was starting to feel irritated.

'I'm just a bit, y'know, "over" the styling thing.'

'How d'you mean?'

'I just think the music should speak for itself a bit more. We shouldn't need loads of hair and make-up and stuff. We're a band, we're musicians . . . I don't know. I'm feeling a bit negative right now.'

Oh God. Billy just didn't get that while one half of his audience might be listening to the music, the other half were ogling the band. And they didn't want to spend forty-five minutes staring at a bunch of kids with dodgy hair in oversized skanky T-shirts sporting bad logo tattoos. Also also also, Billy just didn't appreciate that if it hadn't been for me remodelling his hair into something decent he never would've ever been in a band with Tony Cruz in the first place. I mean, I'm not claiming to be all-powerful or anything but I practically MADE my cousin with the haircut I gave him a couple of years ago. Billy had left Year 9 a World of Warcraft geek and came back in Year 10 a fully formed Post-rock God courtesy of *moi*.

'Fine,' I said. 'I'll sort the styling with Tony. You can join in or not.'

Then I did a mini-flounce and hung up on him. And then I felt guilty and texted him back.

SD: Sorry about hang-up – bad day at the office
Billy: ?
SD: Evil genius hairmeister won't sign my comp form
Billy: Wot u gonna do?
SD: Wait til Saturday . . .

When I arrived at the salon on Saturday, the form was neatly folded in my pocket, waiting to be signed. I swear my hand was on the form as I went into the back office, I swear my mouth was opening to ask Dariusz 'The Question' . . . just as the first customer arrived. At

8.50 a.m. Early. A whole ten minutes early.

'I hear a knocking on the door, Sadie!' said Dariusz. 'Are you going to greet the customer? Or am I going to have to fire your butt already?'

I greeted the customer. And the next one. And the next one. And so by Saturday at 7.05 p.m. I was still greeting customers and the form was still neatly folded in my pocket waiting for a signature.

Misha was right; Dariusz was the best. He was going to go far with the rate he worked and the number of clients he saw. The only trouble was that we might all die of exhaustion in the process.

That day alone I'd done three full heads of highlights, and I'd had Dariusz breathing down my neck at every step of the process. His method of teaching was harsh and relied on repetition. He had made me re-do all the foils for the first head simply because they weren't quite straight enough. He had made me re-condition a client's hair because, as he said, 'I can tell that the hair is begging for more moisture – trust me, I can sense this without even laying a hand on the client. That hair is dry. It needs a drink.'

On top of this I'd done one half-head, a semi-permanent, one straightening, one 'hair up' and a child's trim, as well as the sweeping, the cleaning, the unblocking of the sinks, all the washes and about four billion cups of coffee. For every client who I gowned and seated I had to tell Dariusz what their face shape was and then list the range of styles that would suit them. My head was full of 'heart-shaped', 'square' and 'triangular' clients. I'd been told that square jaws required softening and that triangular heads required fringes. I had cramp in the mouth from offering customers copies of *Heat* with a smile, and my tongue was nearly bleeding from rolling my 'r's when I said the word 'brrrrush' as each new client appeared.

As we neared closing time that evening, my unopened sandwich was still in my bag, as was my unanswered phone, and my unsigned form was folded neatly in my pocket waiting to be signed. Plus I was supposed to be meeting Tony and Billy five minutes ago for my band-styling date.

There was a rap on the door.

'We're closed,' I heard Dariusz's voice call out.

Unlike Misha, who still had couple of customers on the go, Dariusz had finished his last head of the day and was running the client's card through the machine.

There was another rap, on the window this time. I looked up and saw with a shock that it was Tony and Billy. I waved at them and mouthed, 'Five minutes.' Even through my anxiety I could see that Tony was looking extra extra hot standing outside the shop. Sometimes I felt sooooo lucky.

Dariusz looked up at me, his black eyes of doom taking in everything.

'It's OK,' I said to Dariusz. 'It's just my cousin Billy and . . .'

'Well, you can go when you have finished,' said Dariusz in his monotone.'

'Thanks, and would you mind signing my form for me?' I tried to sound casual. 'It's just –'

'One moment please . . .' said Dariusz, doing his best *talk to the hand* gesture. He was booking in the next appointment for the client.

'It's just that you are going to ruin my life,' I muttered under my breath.

I finished sweeping up, took the broom down to the cupboard and retrieved my coat and bag. My mobile was buzzing – it was Billy, demanding to know how much longer I planned to be.

'Why do you even care? I thought you were 'over' styling!' I whispered.

'You're our mascot,' said Billy. He sounded cheerful for once, like he was actually smiling not sighing. 'Hurry up! We're on in less than two hours.'

'I'm rushing! I'm rushing!' I said. 'It's just really hard to leave.'

'Huh?'

Billy wasn't getting it. So then I dredged my memory for World of Warcraft-speak.

'OK. Imagine that this salon is actually Black Rock Depths and my boss is a Dark Iron Dwarf.'

Billy got it. He rang off. Sometimes only geek-speak would do.

I needed to get to the next level in real life now, and for me to do that Dariusz had to sign the form. The deadline was Wednesday. It was my quest and he was not going to stand in my way.

'Dariusz,' I said, approaching the desk again, seeing that his client had finally left. 'This just needs your signature here.' I pointed at the spot on the paper.

He looked up at me and scowled, and as he did so

my phone buzzed, and at the same moment there was another rap on the door.

'What is going on? Some of us are trying TO WORK HERE . . .' Dariusz raised his Dalek-voice, stood up from the desk and yanked open the shop door. This was not going well. In WoW terms, I was dead. A wisp. In the real world eBay was calling.

But then there was a hesitation. And then I heard Dariusz shout. And he no longer sounded angry.

'Enrico!'

'Dariusz!'

And then the two of them were hugging one another and slapping each other on the back like long-lost family or something.

'So, I have wonderful Sadie here. Look!' said Dariusz, pointing at me like I wasn't this irritating trainee who kept asking him to sign forms at inconvenient moments. 'And you sent her to me!' he went on. 'She just appeared last Saturday! Like an ANGEL.'

Huh?

'How's it going?' said Enrico to me. He was red in the face like he was blushing or something, and he looked at me and I nearly passed out of course because he is so extremely hot with his square jaw and dark skin and green eyes and . . .

'Oh, it's going fine,' I said slightly warily. 'I mean it's hard work and it's really busy and . . .'

Then I realised that neither Enrico nor Dariusz was listening to me. They were just too caught up in being so pleased to see one another. They went into this whole conversation about people I'd never heard of and places I'd never been, and it was kind of annoying, the way they totally fried me. Like I didn't exist. Like they were the only people in the room.

'I've come to drag Sadie away, you slave driver,' said Enrico to Dariusz eventually. 'She's styling my brother's band tonight. We're running late.' He checked his watch and grinned at me, like he finally remembered I was there. 'They're on at nine.'

'You have a little brother?' said Dariusz, like Tony was five years old or something and we hadn't had this conversation a week ago. 'I never knew this about you.'

'Sure,' said Enrico, 'and he has a gig and I said I'd drive the gear over. Wanna come down? We'll be at the Royal.'

'Sure thing, sure thing,' said Dariusz. He was smiling

so much I thought his lips might crack.

So then I had one of my few genius moments of inspiration . . .

'Dariusz,' I said right in front of Enrico, 'before I go could you sign the thing?'

I waited. I was on tenterhooks. I was on shpilkas. What can I say? My hands shook as I handed him my competition form for the Thames Gateway Junior Apprentice Hairdresser (or Barber) of the Year Award. All I needed was his signature and life would begin again.

'Sure, sure,' said Dariusz Zengelis, like he'd be simply delighted to do this one thing for me. Like he was so glad I'd asked him. So he scribbled something on the form and I swear I could have asked him to sign a cheque for a couple of grand over to me and he'd have done it right that second.

I'd totally stooged him. And my life was back on track.

15

That's The Kid I Was Talking About

The trainee hairdresser (or barber) should be encouraged to experiment with colour and style wherever possible, on fellow students and friends, thereby improving the skill-set as well as developing creativity.

Guideline 15: Thames Gateway Junior Apprentice Hairdresser (or Barber) of the Year Award

Wow. Rushing off to style my boyfriend's band – it sounds glamorous right?

Wrong.

Wronger than wrong.

In fact: wrong number.

Wrong room.

Wrong time of the month.

Wrong-o-pedia.

The 'dressing room' that Rock Dove crowded into

was pretty much the broom cupboard. The pub where they were appearing had generously tacked a wonky mirror tile on to the wall, supplied a plastic chair with a wobbly leg, hung a filthy net curtain over the window and finished the whole look off with a high-wattage naked light bulb.

'Ooh, glamour!' said Dariusz. 'Takes me right back!'

Oh yes, Dariusz Zengelis, my freaky-deaky, sadistic, robotic boss had tagged along, promising to be my assistant for the evening while I styled Rock Dove. It was so weird that you couldn't make it up.

In actuality, Dariusz took over the styling completely. I have to be honest and say that what he did for the band *was* totally genius, hair and make-up-wise. He ignored what the client (in this case five boys with no unifying vision or sense of style whatsoever) might want or need, and imprinted his own vision entirely. For one thing he managed to persuade the two least interesting members of Rock Dove – the Trotman twins – to have pink bolts of lightning across their hair and eyes. This involved an SFX Crazy Colour spray with matching silicone-based face paint, which Dariusz 'happened' to have in his Montreal 4 Tier XL Mobile Aluminium

Stylist's Trolley he 'happened' to have brought with him. He then outlined the lightning bolts with adhesive pink diamonds and persuaded Alfy Trotman, who generally favoured unwashed, dinge-grey skatewear and who was famous for dribbling out of the left side of his mouth when he played drums, to wear a false eyelash with an arc of silver eyelid-jewels.

'All right, mate,' said Alfy, 'if you think it'll fit with the general *look* of the band then I'll do it.'

'Well,' said Dariusz, who up until about twenty minutes before had never even heard of Rock Dove, 'I know your work, and in my head *this*' (he gestured to the pink lightning bolts) 'is how you sound.'

Oh, purrrrleaze.

'What about me?' said Alfy's twin Jimmy from under his pink lightning bolt. 'Why does he get an eyelash?'

'Quit moaning!' said Dariusz. 'And hold still while I henna your elbows.'

Miraculously this seemed to do the trick and Jimmy retreated into his usual silent stupor.

While Dariusz fixed on diamonds and drew elaborate tattoos, I sprayed the tips of Tony's hair blue like I always did and which I thought added to his general hotness. Tony was my boyfriend and I was determined to style him without 'assistance'. Billy, however, refused absolutely any attempt at being styled. He really was 'over styling'. It was like he had developed a political stance on it overnight.

'What you don't realise,' I said to Billy, while he allowed me to tease some of the wax out of the ends of his hair so it didn't lie quite so flat, 'is that your hairstyle is actually made you in the first place.'

'What?'

'I got you out of Geekdom Hell, Billy, and you know it,' I said.

I could hear the Trotman Twins sniggering behind me.

'I mean I'm not blowing my own trumpet here too much, but you wouldn't even be in a band if it wasn't for that haircut I gave you end of Year 9.'

'I'm not denying it was a good haircut, Sade, it's just . . .'

'Do not underestimate the power of a good haircut!' I stared at the Trotman Twins with their lightning bolts. 'That hair is mutagen to you ninjas.'

'I play guitar,' said Billy defiantly. 'No frills. Just the

music. The hair's fine, Sadie. We're done here.' And he stood up.

What was with him?

'Well, you'll have to turn your back to the audience,' said Dariusz bossily, 'or people will think you belong in another band.'

'Fine with me,' Billy muttered. More weird.

I had never seen my cousin so mardy. His mouth was turned down like he could spit vinegar. The band looked a bit of a shambles with four of them styled to the nines and one of them looking like he'd just got out of bed, but I have to be honest and say that the lack of styling certainly didn't affect Billy's performance any. To be totally fair about it, when they thrashed into their first number Billy's guitar playing outstripped the rest of Rock Dove, and his refusal to be styled singled him out even more. But then my attention turned to Tony and I don't mind admitting it stuck there for a while.

Whenever Tony starts to sing my heart stops beating for a few seconds. My chest goes real tight and I get genuine brain freeze. It doesn't last long, but it's almost like fear – fear that it's not going to be totally great. Which of course it always is. Tony even manages to lean when he sings. He doesn't lean against anything in particular, he puts his head back and closes his eyes and he looks really intense, and my legs feel like wobbly jellies and I wonder why oh why did Tony pick me out of everyone he could go out with? I feel like the luckiest girl alive – I swear, and I pray that he'll never realise that I'm just this small, insecure hair geek.

This particular evening the crowd were a weird bunch. Rock Dove generally played school crowds – teenage parties, that kind of thing – but tonight it was an older audience, pub regulars and some kids from the year above and college too. They didn't seem so fussed with Tony's performance, but whenever Billy played solo they got quite keen.

'That's the kid I was talking about,' said one of the guys next to me.

His mate nodded in an approving sort of way. I saved this up to tell Billy at the end of the gig. He'd be pleased with that. It was always good to pass on a compliment, even if you didn't fully understand it yourself – which I didn't. I mean, Billy could play a guitar. But, y'know, it *was* just a guitar. It wasn't like he stood at the front of the stage and looked intense and leaned against nothing and closed his eyes and sang and made you want to scream, '*You are soooooo cool.*'

The problem was that at the end of the gig when I wanted to go tell him the compliment, Billy was nowhere to be seen. He just vanished. He wasn't backstage with Tony standing under the bare light bulb discussing Rock Dove's performance in depth, which is generally what he does after a gig. He wasn't at the bar sipping a coke, which is the other thing he does after a gig. He'd gone.

'He's gone,' said Tony, who was on his way out to Enrico's car carrying a bunch of wires and guitars. 'He said he had stuff to do. I said I'd shift his gear.'

'Oh,' I said. 'I'm not sure what's got into him. He's gone a bit weird.'

Tony looked uncomfortable.

'Or is it just me?' I said.

'No, you're right – he does seem a bit . . . distracted right now,' said Tony. 'Damn – left my mobile upstairs in the dressing room.'

'I'll get it,' I said.

'See if my brother's there while you're at it!' Tony called after me. 'I'd quite like to get out of here. You look like you could use some TLC and I know I could.'

Tony and his TLC. Like that would ever work out. But you never knew; perhaps we might actually manage it this time, what with Billy off the scene and all.

I got to the door of the dressing-room-broom-cupboard and, without bothering to put on the light, I swung the door open and marched in. Over by the window, two figures were making out, backlit by the street lamp. They did not spring apart as I entered – they were way too engrossed in each other.

'Sorry,' I muttered to no one in particular and let the door close again.

The odd thing was that one of the figures was Enrico de Cruz, Tony's brother, and the other was Dariusz Zengelis, my boss.

16

Return of the Worry Crinkle

The trainee hairdresser (or barber) should ask for honest feedback from employers and colleagues. This will enable him/her to settle well into a new job and improve technical skills.

Guideline 16: Thames Gateway Junior Apprentice Hairdresser (or Barber) of the Year Award

Three thoughts went through my head all at the same time as I raced back down to the car where Tony was waiting.

One thought was pure evil: Aimée Price was totally barking up the wrong tree with Dariusz Zengelis. Dariusz Zengelis wasn't interested in Aimée Price. In fact he wasn't interested in girls. Period.

The second thought made me uncomfortable: Did Tony know about Enrico and Dariusz? And if so, why hadn't he told me? Why hadn't *anyone* told me? Maybe even Billy knew . . . Did they all think I was too young? Too innocent? Too dumb, maybe, to be entrusted with that information? An old insecurity prickled down my spine – Tony didn't really like me; I was just OK till he found someone better. He felt sorry for me. I had no friends. I was very short. I had this weird tremor when I got nervous. I was obsessed with hair. Why would anyone fancy me exactly?

And finally there was a thought that rocked my entire world: Exactly why did I have my job at Stylee Stylee, Roman Road? *Was* it because I'd done a great demonstration on Venus? Or was it because as soon as Dariusz heard that I knew Enrico he just had to have me in his salon, talent or no talent, in the hope that Enrico might pop by? Maybe if I'd trashed Venus's hair he'd have given me the job anyway. Maybe I *had* trashed it. Maybe Aunt Lilah was right all along: I needed to go back to sweeping and washing and nothing more for the time being because I couldn't be trusted. Florence was just trying to be encouraging. She didn't really think I was up to the competition, but she was a teacher so she had to make it look like she knew what she was doing. So maybe Enrico had been way more than my trump card as far as Dariusz was concerned. Maybe Enrico was the *only* reason I had that job.

All of these thoughts scrambled through my head so that it ached with the effort of torturing myself.

'You OK?' said Tony when I joined him outside. He looked concerned.

'Sure!' I said a bit too brightly, 'I couldn't find your mobile though.'

'S'all right – turns out I had it in my jacket,' he said. 'Are you sure you're OK? You look kinda ghosty.'

Clearly my face was betraying me.

Tony put his arm around me and I tried to concentrate on the moment and banish the thoughts I was having, especially the one about being a sympathy date. It actually physically hurt to think that Tony hadn't trusted me with some information, that by omitting to tell me something he had lied. Lying. It was one of those rules, wasn't it? I mean, there are no rules in relationships, but lying was definitely up there. You don't go out with a liar because who knows what else they might be lying about? But Tony wasn't a liar. Surely not. He was Tony. He was my boyfriend. I needed to stop the negative thoughts.

'You were great tonight,' I said, gazing up at him and trying desperately to manufacture a good feeling.

'Crowd weren't that into it though,' he said. 'Not really the right venue maybe. Dunno. Just didn't feel right. Ah, here's our roadie.'

It was Enrico, looking just as cute as ever. Not a hair out of place to suggest that he'd recently been making out with the guest stylist.

'Where's Dariusz?' asked Tony, getting into the back seat with me.

'Oh, he had to go,' said Enrico. 'People to see, bands to style.'

Cute boys to make out with.

I looked around at Tony. Maybe he was all wide-eyed innocence. There was always a possibility that he had no clue as to what was going on with his brother and my boss. And it wasn't down to me to say anything, but I didn't want to keep secrets from Tony either. Then I'd be the liar. He could already read in my face that there was something wrong. I ran my fingertips over my forehead, trying to erase the furrow that formed whenever I was troubled about something. My worry crinkle. It gave me away.

'Are you really OK?' he whispered in my ear as Enrico drove us back. 'You're very quiet. Did we stink this evening? Is that it?'

'No!' I said, 'You were good. You were better than good. The crowd stank, but you guys ripped it. Truly.'

It was while Enrico and I were unloading the car, and Tony was safely out of earshot, that Enrico said, 'Did you find what you were looking for by the way Sadie?' And he winked at me.

'What d'you mean?'

He looked straight at me, so that there could be no doubt as to what he was saying and he smiled. 'I mean in the broom cupboard.'

'Um.' So I'd been seen.

'With the light off.' He raised his eyebrows.

'Err . . .'

'It's OK,' said Enrico, 'It's not a secret.'

I really did not know what to say. It was a new experience for me, being lost for words.

'Tony knows about me and Dariusz. So you don't have to, y'know, worry about having to tell him or not having to tell him – or whatever it is that you're worrying about.'

So Tony did know.

SO TONY KNEW, DID HE?

'So you know,' I said to Tony as soon as we were alone.

'I know what?' said Tony. 'I know a lot of things.'

'About Enrico and Dariusz.'

I was stony-faced now. I'd got over being insecure and I was angry. I felt as if something large was bowling towards me and I had to run at it before it ran over me.

It was clear to me tonight that I was the only person who didn't know about Enrico and Dariusz and I wanted to know why. I was stuck right in the middle of it. I was the bait. Why had nobody bothered to tell me?

'Oh that!' said Tony, laughing and nodding. 'That's old news. That's all over.'

'Well it didn't look like it was all over this evening,' I said.

'How d'you mean?'

'They were making out in the broom cupboard.'

'Were they indeed? Devils. Well it's all over bar the broom cupboard then. Actually it was all over at the start of the summer, but Dariusz still lives in hope. That's what Enrico says.'

I looked away. He wasn't getting it, was he? I was going to have to spell it out. I turned back to him.

'Tony . . .'

'So *that's* why you've got a face on you tonight!' said Tony. He sounded really . . . off. It was the first time I'd ever heard him sound like that.

'Well . . .'

'You think I should have told you about Enrico!'

'Yes I do, as a matter of fact!'

'Why? Why is it important to you who my brother goes out with? Have you got some kind of problem with it?'

'It wouldn't be important – I wouldn't have cared less who Enrico snogged and I wouldn't have a problem with it,' I said, realising with a shock that this was turning into an argument. 'Unless –'

'Unless what?' Tony snapped.

'Let me finish. Unless I started thinking that the reason I'd been given this job wasn't because I was any good at it, but because my boss has the hots for your brother.'

There was a pause. Tony had his mouth open like he was all ready to say something and then he shut it again. I couldn't believe this was happening. We'd never argued before – this was our first! And now it was all going horrible over something I was totally in the right about. Wasn't I?

'I think you're being . . . OTT about this,' he said eventually, 'and unbelievably selfish.'

'On what planet am I being OTT and selfish? You've lied to me about something that was actually pretty important.'

'I did not lie to you, Sadie.'

'Well, technically no, but you deliberately didn't tell me something that was important.'

'Why d'you think I did that? Hmm? Have you thought about why I might not want to broadcast all over town who my brother is or isn't seeing?'

'I wasn't asking you to broadcast it all over town – I was asking you to be honest with *me*. Just with ME! Can't you see that?'

Tony nodded. But he wasn't agreeing with me. He was just gearing up for his next point.

'The trouble is, you can only see *you* in all this,' said Tony. 'Think about my brother's feelings. Why should Enrico have to tell you he had a thing with

Dariusz? Why is it relevant?'

'It's not relevant,' I said, 'unless you're working for that guy. Unless you feel like someone's doing you a favour because they're after something else, rather than giving you a job because you deserve it. I don't want a favour!' I said. 'Well, not a dishonest favour. And anyway, it's not a favour. It looks like one, but actually I feel as if I'm caught up in someone else's game here. All I wanted was an apprenticeship so I could enter the competition . . .'

'*The competition! The competition!* All you care about is that competition. Can't you see that there's something more important at stake here when we're talking about my brother's private life? He is entitled to one, isn't he?'

Tony was shouting now. There were small pockets of moisture forming in the corners of his eyes. I couldn't tell if they were tears of rage or of disappointment at the fact that we were yelling at one another for the very first time. There was a part of me that wanted to reach out and hold him and kiss him and sort this out calmly, but there was a bigger part that felt like yelling too because I'd been made to look like a fool. Because everyone knew something and I didn't. Because there was a conspiracy. Because . . .

'If you'd have just been honest with me and told me Enrico was more than the trump card – that Enrico was going to actually get me the job – then I could have chosen to have played him or not. But you never told me. You never told me! I thought they were just college mates because that's what Enrico told me and he told me in front of you and you never contradicted him.'

'Yeah,' said Tony, 'well he's my brother and, y'know what, Sadie, I have to respect him too. You wouldn't understand this. You don't have any brothers or sisters – you don't know what it's like to have a regular family.'

That was it. He'd completely crossed the line.

17

A Really Bad Evening

The trainee hairdresser (or barber) should ensure that they are fully briefed on information relating to salon facilities, equipment and customer demands. A well-informed trainee is better able to carry out their work, to the best of their abilities.

Guideline 17: Thames Gateway Junior Apprentice Hairdresser (or Barber) of the Year Award

Of course Billy chose just that moment to turn up. He banged on the front door and Tony left the room to answer it. He was probably happy to have an excuse.

'Hi,' said Billy, drifting into Tony's room and picking up a guitar. 'S'up.' He stared from me to Tony. I had my hands on my hips and Tony was staring fixedly at the ground like he couldn't stand to look at me. 'Not interrupting anything, am I?'

'No, you aren't interrupting,' I said. 'I was just leaving anyway.'

I half wanted Tony to stop me.

'Fine!' he said, and he looked me right in the eye like he was seeing me for the first time or something. Maybe he was. Maybe he'd just realised what a childish, selfish, talentless loser he was going out with. I'd always known it. Wasn't I always telling him? Wasn't I always asking him why he liked me? So now he knew I was right.

'Billy'll walk me home, won't you, Bill?' I said, putting my coat on and going towards the door. I could feel little itty bitty tears beneath my eyelids that were threatening to fall if I didn't get a move on.

'I was going to catch up with Tony,' said Billy. 'That's kind of why I'm here.'

'Billy, how 'bout you catch up with Tony later?' I said, almost pleading. 'After you've walked me home.'

'OK,' said Billy, although he looked puzzled.

I went out of Tony's room, all the while waiting for him to say something.

But he didn't. And neither did I. There was nothing to say that covered how I felt.

The whole evening had been a disaster. My boyfriend had finally realised that I was a loser weirdo. Added to this my job was a sham and my future had been compromised. Again. All in one night.

Of course Billy, still oblivious to the situation, decided to be more obscure and silent on our walk back than I'd ever known him before. I silently mopped up the tears that were spilling down my face freely now, mixing in with my mascara and dripping off the end of my nose. I was grateful for the darkness.

'I feel like everything's changing . . . y'know, Sadie,' Billy said eventually, after a series of long sighs.

'No, I don't know, Billy. You're going to have to explain what you mean.' I sniffed.

I was feeling impatient with him. I mean, how much of a mess did I need to be in before he actually noticed? Tony had accused *me* of being unaware of other people's feelings – but Billy was being a total 'Me-man'.

'It's like I have all these strong feelings and they're kind of going in the wrong direction,' Billy continued.

'How's that?' It was so irritating – I do love my cousin, don't get me wrong, but I had no idea what he was talking about and I was so tired and confused by the evening's events that I could barely manage to listen. But his voice was becoming urgent and so I tried really hard to focus on what he was saying.

'I mean, I want them, these feelings, to go to one place – where they *should* go, where they're *supposed* to go – but they keep going somewhere else. And now I have to say something, and I have to be true to myself . . .'

'What feelings are you talking about, Billy?'

'I've been *trying* to tell you – I've tried to be truthful.' He was struggling to get the words out. 'I've tried so many times, but I just couldn't and now I'm going to . . . and you're going to be shocked . . .'

And then I realised what he was trying to tell me. *That everything was changing . . . that his feelings were going in the wrong direction . . . that he had to be true to himself . . .* that HE WAS IN LOVE WITH ENRICO TOO!

It was so clear now. I was the dimmest person on the planet, who had failed to spot my cousin falling for Tony's brother. While I had flitted around being a band stylist that evening, I had imagined myself to be the only person in the broom cupboard who thought that Enrico was hot – when in fact I was at the back of a queue that included my boss and my cousin!

I decided to put him out of his misery.

'It's OK,' I said. 'I know. I figured it out.'

'You did?' said Billy. 'You figured it out and you don't hate me? What about Tony – does he know?'

'No!' I said. 'But I'm sure he won't mind. I mean, it won't matter to him.'

'It *will* matter to him. He'll be devastated!' said Billy, 'I've been trying to tell him for weeks now . . . ever since everything happened . . . but I just couldn't find the words.'

'Everything *happened*?' I said, '*What's* happened exactly?' I mean, hadn't I just seen Enrico and Dariusz in the broom cupboard that evening? Had Enrico and Billy already . . .? I felt defensive for my cousin. I felt angry. 'You have to tell me,' I said firmly, 'if something's happened.'

'I was approached . . .' said Billy.

Now I really was lost.

'OK, Billy – what are we talking about here?'

'The band!' he said.

'What d'you mean, *the band*?'

'Rock Dove! I mean I'm leaving. I've been asked to join Interpol. They're a really cool band with a

148

possible deal on the table. I thought you said you'd figured it out . . .?'

'I thought I had,' I said. 'But I figured it out all wrong.'

So Billy was leaving Rock Dove. This was shaping up to be a knock-out evening.

'You're right, Tony *will* be devastated,' I said, and then I began to cry quite openly. I was crying because I felt sorry for Tony and because Tony had lied to me and made me feel stupid and called me a freak, and because I loved watching the band and because the band wouldn't be the band any longer, and because my job wasn't a real job and because and because and because . . . Hot tears of pity, anger and confusion.

'Have you guys had a fight?' said Billy.

'How d'you work that one out?' I sniffed.

Of course I shouldn't have been mad at Billy – none of this was his fault. But then it occurred to me that maybe it was.

'Wait a minute,' I said. 'D'you know about "The Enrico and Dariusz Show"?'

'What d'you mean?' said Billy. 'I mean I know they're mates – Enrico said so and that was pretty obvious this evening, but they're like the Odd Couple, aren't they? I mean, Dariusz is way older and he's kind of annoying. Bossy.'

'Billy,' I said, 'they used to go out.'

'OK?' said Billy. 'I never knew *that*.'

'And Dariusz is still holding a candle for Enrico – well, it's more like a flaming Olympic torch.'

'OK,' said Billy, 'I never knew that either – but what does it have to do with anything? I mean why'd you and Tony have a fight about it?'

'Because Tony never told me,' I said. 'And I don't know why, and then I started wondering if that was the reason I got the job in the first place.'

'How d'you mean?'

'I mean, what could *possibly* have persuaded Dariusz to give me a job in his salon when he knew that I was friends with Mr Better-Looking-Than-God?'

'Sadie,' said Billy, 'he gave you that job because you do good hair. Dariusz is a pro – he wouldn't give a job to someone who was going to annihilate his reputation.'

'I'm just not sure you're right,' I said.

'But Tony should have been straight with you in the first place,' Billy continued, 'because I can see how this looks. I mean, it's like if Tony told me to get an audition with this other band and to mention his name because they were "mates", and I did and they gave me the gig – after they heard me play – and then I found out that the lead singer fancied Tony and thought he might come by . . .'

I didn't like this analogy one bit.

'I'm not liking this,' I told him. '*Does* the lead singer of Inter-whatever-they're-called fancy Tony?'

'Interpol? Which lead singer we talking about?'

'The one in the band Tony told you to audition for.'

'He didn't – this is just scenario! It's hypothetical. Tony would never do that.'

'No, Tony would never do that,' I agreed, although I didn't agree 100 per cent like I would've done the day before. Before I realised Tony had lied to me.

'So, yeah, I can see how this looks to you,' said Billy, 'but you just have to get over it, because like I said, Dariusz wouldn't have given you the job if you were useless.'

'Well, I can't just get over it,' I said. 'I *can* get over the fact that I'm going to have to work doubly hard in that job to prove to myself that I deserve it, but I can't get over that Tony didn't tell me the whole truth. That he lied to me. And that he thinks that's OK and that he basically called me a freak for thinking otherwise.'

'So what does that mean – if you can't get over it?' asked Billy, as we got to my building.

I wanted to pre-empt Tony. I wanted to pre-empt the text message that would change everything; the hollow phone call that I knew would rock my world. For twelve months I'd known it was inevitable that one day he would see me for who I was and wonder why we were together. That moment had just happened.

The only control I had over this situation was to act first.

'It means we're breaking up,' I said to Billy. 'It means that me and Tony are finished.'

18

Life Begins Again

Judges at the competition will be on the lookout for the competitor's self-motivation and the ability to cope with potential disaster in the salon.

Guideline 18: Thames Gateway Junior Apprentice Hairdresser (or Barber) of the Year Award

Life was this white blank page.

Wait a minute, no it wasn't.

The morning after I woke up from the Really Bad Evening, life was a soiled grey rag.

I checked my phone. There was nothing. I checked my email too. One empty mailbox. In the end, I hadn't sent the text. Hadn't made the call. I decided to wait and see. But he hadn't texted or called either. In fact, he'd probably done the breaking up thing in typical style – by doing absolutely nothing. Right now, Tony was probably waking up feeling good, released – like this great big weight had been lifted off his shoulders. Like he was free again. He wouldn't feel like that when Billy told him his news about leaving the band, so that was some comfort at least.

It was time for me to begin again too, I decided. I did not need anyone. I crushed my instinct to log into www.girlswholoveboyswhoplayWoW.com and look for Groovechick2 and tell her everything. I didn't even need her. I was marble. I was impervious to feeling. I was a Hairdressing Machine who was going to win that competition.

I unfolded my application form with Dariusz's scrawl in the signature box. It was complete. I'd rewritten my statement, I had my sealed envelope from Florence and my boss had signed the paper.

I took out a clean white envelope and began to transcribe the address, which was somewhere in Kent, and then I glanced at the closing date once again.

22nd October.

22nd October. I checked my phone. It said Sunday 21st October. That meant that the deadline was tomorrow! And I thought that the deadline was on Wednesday. How many times had I looked at that form?

How could the deadline be tomorrow? How could they make a deadline a Monday? It meant that you had to have posted the form on the Saturday at the latest. Which I guess was fairly reasonable . . . But still . . .

'Well, it *is* tomorrow, Sadie Nathanson,' I said in my Aunt Lilah's voice.

I said it how she would say it. Like, '*This is what happens when you misbehave in my salon, young lady. You get what you deserve.*'

I left the form on the table at the end of my bed and got back under the duvet. There was really nothing to come out for any more. There was no Tony, there was no real job and now there was no competition. I pulled the duvet right over my head just as Mum poked her head around the door.

'Oh dear,' she said. 'That bad?'

'It is,' I said from the under the duvet. Because, well, it actually *was* that bad.

'It's rather early for everything to have gone wrong already in the day,' said Mum.

I pulled the duvet down slightly. 'It started last night.'

I could feel the tears beginning to burn again behind my eyes. Why couldn't I just be a Hairdressing Machine?

After all, aren't these the moments that sort the salon juniors from the senior stylists? The worst moments – the moments when you hit rock bottom – are how characters are built. To get through them requires grim determination, struggles against personal demons, triumph over adversity and all those other clichés that you read about in those lame-o *Hello* interviews. If my life was a musical I'd be singing one of those 'I'll show 'em' numbers. This was the lowest I was going to get – and of course the positive spin on this was that I must now be on my way up.

The only trouble was that I wasn't in *The Sound of Music,* having been sacked from the convent and about to fall madly in love with an Austrian baron and seven children. I was under a duvet in Hackney, East London, and my mum was standing there going, 'Well, I hope it's nothing physical. I must admit I thought that herring of Aunty Rita's tasted a bit off on Friday night. Gave me terrible heartburn.'

'I'm fine, really,' I said, slamming back the duvet.

Is it possible to slam a duvet? It felt like it was. And I did.

I didn't want to spend the day hiding from the world

in my bed, because tomorrow I would have to get up and go to college and everyone would be like, 'Oooh did you get your competition form in?' and then at school on Tuesday they'd be all like, 'Ooh, is it true you and Tony have split up?' and, 'Ooh – is it true that Billy's leaving Rock Dove?'

'I feel fine,' I said to Mum. I was gulping and swallowing those wretched tears, defying them to escape down my face.

'OK!' said Mum. 'If you say so!' and she raised her eyebrows at me as she left the room.

I picked up the competition form again. It needed to get to Ashford – in Kent. Bough Beeches, where Abe lived, was in Kent too. An idea popped into my head. I could get to Bough Beeches and ask Abe to drive me the rest of the way. I could deliver it by hand and make the deadline. It was a brilliant idea.

I loved the idea of seeing Abe today. Abe wouldn't pry. He'd talk to me about work. He'd listen to me – hell, maybe I'd even tell him about Tony and the whole twisted scenario. Maybe he was just the person to talk to. A total outsider with no agenda other than my best interests. I would do it.

Suddenly I was Julie Andrews. I was Joan of Arc. I was Susan Bloody Boyle. Suddenly Sunday was a day where everything was possible. I was getting out of bed and putting on my clothes and texting Abe, ignoring the three other texts – all from Billy and none from Tony.

'I think I might go and see Abe today, if that's OK with you,' I said to Mum.

'That's fine, love,' Mum said vaguely. 'You do look a bit peaky though.'

'I'm OK,' I said. 'Physically I'm fine.' Emotionally was a whole other story.

'Well, I'm sure I'll be the last to know if there's anything else going on,' said Mum.

And there it was. Always some comment to make me feel worse.

'Why d'you have to say stuff like that?' I said. 'I mean, if there was actually something wrong d'you think I'd tell you when you're so . . . sarcastic?'

Mum stared at me. 'Well is there, Sadie? Is there something the matter?'

I paused. Maybe it would be better to just tell her. Sound her out. Why go running to Abe? I hesitated. It was so tempting.

But then I knew with utter certainty that if I told Mum, she'd just call up Aunt Lilah who'd probably say, 'Did she actually think she got that job on merit?' and Uncle Zé would give me the lecture about how 'Boys Are Only After One Thing' and I'd feel as if I'd gone backwards a whole year. I just couldn't face it.

'I'm fine, really,' I said. 'Just tired.'

I did accept a lift to the station from Mum though, and by 10.30 I was on a train to Bough Beeches, despite the fact that Abe hadn't yet called me back. Hell! I decided to risk going anyway. It felt so good to be leaving London and my messy life behind me.

I fidgeted all the way down on the train. There was a finger mark on the competition envelope from where my hands had sweated. I continually checked my mobile. For Abe. For Tony. I began to feel that everything might be all right.

So sorry Tony's might say. And then maybe I'd call him and maybe we'd make up . . . But then come Saturday I'd have to go into Stylee Stylee and Dariusz would be there, smiling like his face was going to crack because if I was in the salon then there was always the chance that Enrico might just stop by. How could I bear that? I tried to stop thinking about it.

At Bough Beeches there was no one at the station – it felt a little chilly and desolate. The usually bright baskets of flowers were dried up and rustling in the breeze and the station building was all locked up. I checked my mobile. There wasn't even a signal out here, let alone a friendly text from Abe. The public phone at the station was out of order, but an old lady pointed me in the direction of a bus that she said went along Weald Lane, which was where Abe lived.

The countryside was really hard to get around compared to London. It was like you could get to some bits and not others unless you had a car or you didn't mind walking miles. I ended up walking miles anyway because the bus driver put me down on Weald Lane without telling me that Weald Lane was about four miles long. Abe was at Number 17, right up the other end, and by the time I realised this the bus had pulled away.

I felt a bit weird ringing Abe's doorbell when I got there. I'd never just turned up unannounced before. His car was parked outside so I knew he had to be around, but he didn't come to the door. I rang the bell again. Then I used the knocker – maybe the bell wasn't working. But nobody came. He clearly wasn't in. Perhaps he was out walking Daisy. Maybe he was away and he'd left his car here. Maybe he was at his girlfriend Sarah's.

I sat down on the front step and thought about my next move. Ashford. I needed to get to Ashford by the end of the day. I had to deliver my form. I stood up and walked to the front gate.

'Sadie?' A voice from a long way off was calling me.

I turned my head. There was Abe, miles down Weald Lane. There was Abe, and someone else who wasn't Sarah, coming along the lane with Daisy the dog. I felt relieved, and then a bit awkward. Like I'd interrupted something. But Abe didn't seem at all bothered, in fact he seemed really pleased by the way he was rushing to greet me.

'Hi Sadie!' he was shouting. 'I just got your text! Really sorry!'

The other someone who wasn't Sarah was now waving at me. It was all a bit weird – I had no idea who she was and yet as she got closer she seemed familiar. I could have sworn I'd seen her before somewhere. And then it came to me when she turned and I saw her hair.

A French plait. It was the same girl I'd collided with on my road when I was ringing Billy last Monday.

'Sadie!' said Abe, holding out his arms to hug me. 'This,' he said, placing his hand on the shoulder of the French-plait girl, 'is Marie.'

19

I Always Wanted a Sister

A positive attitude at all times is a prerequisite for the successful trainee hairdresser. Determination to follow something through is another quality judges will be on the lookout for.

Guideline 19: Thames Gateway Junior Apprentice Hairdresser (or Barber) of the Year Award

'Hey . . . b-b-but I've seen you before!' I said.

Was this some kind of a bizarre coincidence? I was shocked and puzzled. I felt like I must have made some kind of a mistake. Somebody must have made a mistake.

Marie looked sheepish. She pulled that cool blonde plait across her mouth, 'I'm a bit embarrassed. Can you forgive me? I'm really not a weirdo.'

'I don't get it,' I said. But now I knew for sure that I had seen her before. Which meant she had stalked me. It was crazy! But she was my half-sister and she'd totally stalked me and I'd seen her before and . . .

'Did you, like, look me up?' I squeaked.

I squeaked because I couldn't manage to talk properly. Because I was shocked. I was amazed. Because this was my half-sister standing in front of me, and I'd seen her before.

'Yup.' She smiled.

'You . . . followed me?'

She didn't have to nod. I totally got it. She'd looked me up so that she could get a good look at me. Because she was curious. Because she was excited. It was pretty out-there behaviour, but sort of wonderful at the same time.

'So you two have met?' said Abe.

'Well, not exactly . . .' I said.

'I looked you up,' said Marie, nodding fiercely now and turning red. 'I looked Sadie up!' she said to Abe.

She'd followed me. My half-sister had actually followed me.

'Abe gave me your address,' Marie continued, 'and I just couldn't wait. I wanted to see what you looked like and so before I knew what I was doing I was outside your building and I went up to your flat and I knocked on the door, but there was no one in . . .'

'It was Monday – Mum was at work . . . I was on my way back . . .'

'So I lost my nerve and then I was walking away, back towards the station, and I saw someone coming along the road and it was you. And you shouted, "It's Sadie!" into your phone and I thought, *OMG it's her – it's my sister!* And here you are and and and . . .!'

'You went to my flat? I never saw you there, but you did stalk me! I saw you in the street!'

'I can't believe I did that. It was like something out of a movie,' Marie put her hands over her mouth. 'I am so embarrassed. I've never done anything like that in my entire life!'

She had been to my flat. She had stalked me. She was my half-sister and I'd noticed her because of her hair. That last bit had to be a good omen, didn't it?

'I love your hair,' I said. 'I noticed it and I completely loved it.'

I was a fine one to talk about stalking. Classic stalking behaviour, collecting hair.

'That's it,' said Abe. 'You've had the seal of approval now, Marie.'

'But I do love your hair,' I said. 'I mean, it's made me want to grow mine long again. Seriously. I'm sort of growing it out of the Cleopatra thing anyway. That French plait – well, it's really neat and sporty and fresh.'

'Thanks,' said Marie. 'Thanks for not minding me being a weirdo creepazoid!' She held out her arms to me and suddenly we were hugging.

'This is amazing!' she said, wiping away tears. 'It's so weird! I lost my father last year and now I've got two new members of my family. Are other people's lives like this?'

'Noooo! I don't think so,' I said.

'We just got lucky I guess,' said Marie.

'That's pretty much how I feel,' I said. 'It's how I felt when Abe first told me about you.'

'I always wanted a sister,' said Marie.

I wanted to say that I did too, but it felt a bit disloyal to Billy somehow. 'I have a cousin who is like my brother,' I said, 'but a sister is something else, isn't it?'

'I'd love to meet the rest of your family,' said Marie. 'Abe says they're great. D'you think I could sometime?'

'Sure. Sure,' I said. Marie was saying all the right things. 'Billy is really keen to meet you too, so is my mum. We should get our mums together maybe.'

Marie didn't say anything. She looked over at Abe.

'Marie's mum's having a hard time over the whole donor thing right now,' Abe explained.

'I think Mum had it all buried so deep for so long that it's almost like it never really happened at all,' said Marie. She looked really sad for a moment.

'It must be very hard,' I said, 'having lost your dad and everything.'

'Yeah, but it's crazy really. It doesn't make me feel like my dad was never my dad, or whatever. I just wish they'd told me before. I would have been fine with it all.'

She was right. Uncle Zé would always be my dad, even now I had Abe. There had never been a 'space' in my life and Abe had never replaced anyone. He had just added to the mix.

We went into the house and pretty soon Sarah popped by. While she chatted with Marie and Abe, I was able to stand back a bit and get a really good look at my sister. She was at least three inches taller than me – clearly the height thing is all Mum's fault – and her hair was fairer than Abe's, but a similar texture – wavy, maybe even curly outside of that plait. She had a heart-shaped face and her skin was darker than it should have been for someone with that colour hair. I mean, she was real lucky with her complexion. Her eyes were brown too, like mine, although a different shape, but then of course there was the hand thing. I had to point it out. I had to mention it.

'Look . . .' I spread my fingers out on the table. Abe spread his and now Marie did the same. Short stubby fingers and a slight tremor.

'Do yours shake like that when you're nervous?' I said.

'Sure,' said Marie. 'I'm always worrying that it's a sign of something terrible.'

'Well, it is,' said Sarah. 'It's a sign that you're related to Abe!'

'I don't mind that!' said Marie. 'I don't mind that one bit!'

'So, Sadie,' said Abe, 'you said in your text that you want a lift to Ashford – is that right? What's it for? It's gotta be important I'm guessing.'

I explained the extreme gravity of the competition situation and how I now needed to hand-deliver the entry form. I didn't bother to go into the complications

I had with my job, my boyfriend, his brother, my boss and my nerdy cousin Billy. I considered it to be a minor miracle that I was up, dressed, in Kent and actually breathing.

'Y'know what?' said Marie. 'Maybe Sadie and I could go to Ashford together – on the train. I'm a couple of stops along in Canterbury. I just feel like there's a load more to say, being that we've only just met and started talking and all. Would that be OK? Ashford really is in my direction anyway.'

'Sure, no problem,' said Abe. 'Is that OK, Sadie?'

Was it OK? It was more than OK.

'It's great,' I said, beaming. And I never beam.

We could both have chatted for England that journey. I mean, we were Olympic standard chat-level. Especially Marie. She was a gold medallist in the chatting department. She was right up there on the top of the podium. She literally didn't stop. She told me about her mum, who was still depressed after being widowed, about her home town, where everybody was really smug (*'Just about the most boring place on the planet – you are so lucky to be in London, Sadie'*), her friends, who were all desperate to leave and go to university, and her dog Mungo, and the dog she had before that, and her guinea pigs that got eaten by a fox when she was a kid, and . . . then the announcement came up for Ashford and it said that we could change here for the Eurostar and go to Paris.

'Wouldn't that be amazing?' said Marie. 'If we just went, "Sod everything – let's just go to Paris!" I would love that. Sisters in Paris!'

'But then I wouldn't get my form in,' I said. 'Hate to put a damper on things, but I can't do Paris because I have a hair competition to enter!' I waved the envelope at her.

'I'll come with you,' said Marie and she grinned at me. 'We'll deliver it together.'

The offices were easy enough to find. Straight down Station Road and then first left into a little muse of characterless red-brick buildings, one of which was Diamond House, the administrative office for the Thames Gateway Junior Apprentice Hairdresser (or Barber) of the Year Award.

'Don't forget to kiss the envelope!' Marie said as I was about to drop the form through the letter box.

'Huh?'

'Oh, it's a thing I always do when I really care about a letter I've written. Like a good luck thing, y'know. I did it when I wrote to Abe. And look – I had good luck!'

Aunty Rita was like that. All superstitions. No hats on beds. No naming of children after the living. Never saying the word 'cancer' without spitting afterwards. The list was endless. But kissing envelopes? This was a new one on me.

But I did it anyway. I kissed the envelope before I posted it. What can I say? I like to fit in. I have no concrete belief system myself. From my vague memory of religious education class I think I'm called a polytheist, which means I tend to pray to different gods depending on what's going on. For example, the night before last I prayed to the God of Virus Software when Mum's laptop went into meltdown, and the week before it was St Martin de Porres, who I found out is the patron saint of hairdressers. St Martin de Porres used to give his fellow monks those cute little monk-dos – Wikipedia tells me they're called 'tonsures', which sounds more like it has to do with the back your throat. But anyway St Martin de Porres does come in useful every now and then. I think I'll dig him out for the competition.

So, back to kissing envelopes. I liked Marie and I wanted her to like me too and that's why I kissed the envelope. It's great getting a new relative, but it's kind of complicated too. I mean, you don't have to get your family that you've had all along to like you, do you? Aunt Lilah doesn't like me right now, but I've never doubted for a second that she loves me. Does that make any sense?

Marie was actually quiet on the walk back to the station in Ashford, having gabbed all the way from Abe's house. I guess she was having a big think about stuff too.

'It's been really really totally super-fantastic to meet you, Sadie,' she said, giving me a hug before she went to her platform to wait for a Canterbury train. 'I hope you don't mind the stalking thing . . . Can I call you and meet up again?'

'Sure. Of course. I would really like you to meet Billy and Mum and To–' I was about to mention Tony, and then the whole of the previous night's bad memory flooded back and it just felt like this deadweight. 'Sure,' I said, 'just give me a call.'

'Good luck with the competition!'

And she was gone. My sister Marie. And I was alone and I was back to thinking about Tony and Dariusz and Billy and Enrico and, well, to be honest I really wish I hadn't because it kind of spoiled everything really.

Of course, Mum was waiting eagerly when I got home, all smiling and grey-toothed. 'How was Abe? Was Sarah there? Has he heard any more from Marie?'

I answered a million questions, except for the one about Marie. Marie was still mine for the moment. Just the fact of her. It was a bit like when I first heard from Abe – when I got that very first letter confirming that he might be my dad. I wouldn't let Mum tell ANYONE. I needed it to just be my thing.

But I wanted to talk about Marie too, because it was exciting and I realised that holding out on Mum was a bit, well, childish. So I changed my mind.

'I met her,' I said calmly and matter-of-factly while we were having tea.

'You *met* her?' said Mum. 'You met Marie?'

'I met her!' I said.

'And and and and . . .' said Mum. She was leaning into my face now. Like she was *in* my soup.

'She was cool!' I said. 'She's the same age and she doesn't live too far away and her mum's having a hard time coming to terms with it all and we look nothing alike.'

'I was just going to ask . . .'

'Except our hands. We have the hand thing . . .'

'Hand thing?'

'Shaky, small, stubby, generally ugly hand thing courtesy of Abe.'

'You and your hand thing!' Mum smiled. 'There's nothing wrong with those hands.'

I thought there was, but I wouldn't swap them anyhow. They were what connected me to Abe and Marie. I was sort of proud of them. If anyone ever remarked on them, I'd say, 'I take after my dad with these hands. My sister has them too.'

No one would ever understand just how good that made me feel!

20

Green Eyed Monster

Physical appearance and presentation are extremely important aspects of a hairdresser's (or barber's) ability to gain the customer's confidence. A hairdresser with a well-groomed appearance can inspire a group of customers wanting to copy their style. This is great for the professional and great for the salon too.

Guideline 20: Thames Gateway Junior Apprentice Hairdresser (or Barber) of the Year Award

Monday morning and still nothing from Tony. No text. No phone call. No rocking up unannounced like he had that time when I'd accused him of kissing Shonna Matthews – so long ago, in a galaxy far, far away. For now it was Radio Silence. And added to that, I was having to listen to Mum telling Aunt Lilah all about Marie over the phone. I kept hearing her say, 'And apparently she's lovely . . . Sadie's thrilled . . . yes – lovely apparently, yes – thrilled . . .'

That was that. Marie was no longer mine.

I stood in front of my stupid Snow White mirror, unsmiling, twisting my hair into a chignon just like Aunt Lilah's. I wasn't going to let the Tony thing or the Marie thing throw me. I was Sadie Nathanson: Hairdressing Machine. Even if I totally lacked raw talent I would make myself good through sheer determination.

At college Aimée Price was wearing gold-effect nail extensions that matched her gold shiny bag, which blended with the gold thread running through her jacket and toned with the gold eyeshadow plastered on to her lids. I wanted to applaud, even though the effect was cheesy as hell. It clearly made her stand out because Florence picked her to do the demo that morning. We were back-combing and Florence was a tiny bit impressed with Aimée's technique because she managed to get the style real tight, so that there was plenty of volume underneath, but you couldn't see the raggedy bits at all. Then she totally pulled the whole thing into a smooth shiny beehive. I'll admit that this showed good technique, although it pained me to think anything good about Aimée Price's ability to do hair.

'Actually Dariusz showed me how to do that the

other day – did he tell you?' Aimée said to me afterwards when we were paired up again and practising on each other's roots. (It bugged me how Florence always insisted on pairing us.)

I shook my head.

'He called me over from Misty's when you'd gone to lunch,' Aimée continued. 'He was on a wedding 'do for someone and he thought I might like to watch and learn.'

It had to be Sally Schaeffer's wedding 'do. I had taken the booking. It was not just 'someone'. *I* HAD TAKEN THE BOOKING. *I* had wanted to watch Dariusz doing that one. It should have been *me* doing the demo today.

A wave of jealousy coursed its way through my body. It prickled down my spine, touching all of my nerve endings. A week ago I would've been a bit envious, but since Saturday night I was totally jealous AND insecure. After all, if Dariusz was giving away his technique secrets to Aimée Price, maybe he saw her as a serious contender – pretty much confirming that I wasn't working in his salon just by virtue of my sheer brilliance. Sure, I was his trainee, but he had barely even mentioned that particular 'do to me. He was finishing up when I'd come back from lunch — actually, I hadn't even *had* lunch. Dariusz had sent me to the Post Office with his stupid product order. The stupid product order that anybody with an ounce of technical nous could generate electronically so that nobody would have to queue in the Post Office and miss the wedding 'do featuring the back-combing technique that Aimée Price got to perfect and so be picked out for special demonstration by Florence.

'Yeah, well, you're barking up the wrong tree with Dariusz,' I said, and the words just came tumbling out. 'I've met his boyfriend.'

There was a couple of minutes' silence. Just enough time for me to realise and to regret what a total bitch I had just been to Aimée Price. In the thick mire of my jealousy was a tiny speck of decency. After all, Aimée Price was only aiming for the same thing I was. She was ambitious and she was determined — just like me. All that *you want something, you go get it girl* was paying off and she was clearly getting good now, although I hated to admit that. She was gaining on me and I couldn't bear it.

I wanted to pee on her parade. I wanted to poop on

her cake. I was still mad at Tony, and if I didn't have a boyfriend, why should she?

'Whateva,' said Aimée. She was blushing fiercely. 'I'm only really interested in the professional tips Dariusz can give me. The other stuff isn't that important. And y'know what?'

I shook my head. I couldn't speak or meet her eye.

'Dariusz was really happy to share those tips with me on Saturday. He doesn't think I'm no slouch potato. You aren't the only one with talent around here, y'know.'

I walked over to the sinks to wash my brush, biting my lip to stop the tears coming. Sadie Nathanson: Hairdressing Machine. Must. Try. Harder.

I texted Billy.

> **SD: Cn u meet me at salon after school? Need ur help**
> **Billy: I left u 3 txt msgs – u never replied & btw; I don't do hair**
> **SD: Sorry sorry sorry. Crisis! Need ur geekism not ur hair**

The salon said CLOSED, but the office light was on and we could see Dariusz in there going around the shelves with his stoopid clipboard, writing down the names of the products for his stoopid ordering system. He wrote longhand and then transcribed it on to the computer, typing one finger at a time.

He didn't want to let us in, of course, but I wasn't taking no for an answer. I got straight to the point.

'We can do that electronically for you so that it's instant,' I said. 'That's why Billy's here.'

'Oh yes, Billy, the backwards guitar player,' said Dariusz, tapping away at his keyboard. 'I don't think I ordered a guitar player though, did I?'

'No,' I said. I was almost used to Dariusz's unsmiling sarcasm by now. 'But Billy's a geek too, and he can set this ordering-thing up for you on your computer.'

'Hmmm,' said Dariusz, 'and how long will this take?'

'I'll be quick,' said Billy. I was lucky he'd turned up. He was frowning. In fact, he was really off with me. He still was smarting from those unreturned texts. Plus he'd probably heard from Aunt Lilah that I'd met Marie and I hadn't even filled him in about that yet. We used to share everything, me and Billy – a little island of sanity in our family. Perhaps he was right – everything *was* changing.

'How much you charge?' Dariusz asked Billy.

'A haircut. A really decent haircut,' said Billy.

Huh?

I stared at my cousin. What was this? *I* was his stylist. I'd taken him from total nerd to almost cool in one easy haircut, even if these days he kept protesting that it was too much style over substance.

Then again, maybe he was right. After all, who was to say I was any good? My current job said nothing about my talent as it turned out, and I'd been fired from my first job for being a hothead. Maybe I was simply a poor hairdresser. Perhaps even Billy could see that. And so he had no loyalty, and therefore no qualms about seeing another hairdresser.

Face it, Nathanson. You stink at everything.

Where Dariusz was concerned my only winning ticket was the people I knew: first Enrico and now Billy. Because you had to hand it to Enrico – it hurt to look at him. And you had to hand it to my cousin Billy – he was amazing on a computer. It took about twenty minutes for him to set everything up.

'Look,' Billy said to Dariusz, 'you have a stock control system as part of your package on your till here.'

'I do?' said Dariusz.

'You do,' said Billy. 'So you can scan the products out as you sell them or use them. Look.' He opened a window on the PC. 'Here's your status now. This is the number of products you have currently.'

'Yuh,' Dariusz looked down at his clipboard. 'Yup this is correct. I typed that all in last week. I was going to update that with these figures here.'

'But you don't need to,' said Billy, 'if you just scan them, like this . . . Then you summarise . . .' He clicked the 'Summary' tab. 'And there's your order.'

"Wow, that's fast.' Dariusz turned to me. 'You're right. It's quicker.'

Quelle surprise and SCORE. I might not be the Great Talent, but Billy had put me on the first rung to making myself indispensable.

'Save it,' continued Billy, 'and *email* it to the wholesaler.' Billy emphasised the word 'email'. I had told him about the pointless queuing in the Post Office.

'OK, Sadie, you win,' Dariusz turned to me. 'It is quicker and it will make me more streamlined and efficient. You totally win.'

Ha! I waited for the 'thank you', but of course it

never came from my unsmiling psycho boss.

Dariusz turned to Billy. 'And now, young man, for your haircut.'

I couldn't help myself. I couldn't stick around for this. I stalked out of the salon and slammed the door behind me.

I had lost my first client.

21

Toasted

The hairdresser (or barber) will undoubtedly make mistakes during his or her career, particularly during the training period. It is rare but entirely possible, when dealing with the application of chemicals to the hair or the use of heat, that mistakes will result in injury to the client.

Guideline 21: Thames Gateway Junior Apprentice Hairdresser (or Barber) of the Year Award

> *Dear Miss Nathanson,*
> *We are pleased to inform you that you are one of the two hundred apprentice hairdressers (or barbers) who have been selected to compete at the Thames Gateway Junior Apprentice Hairdresser (or Barber) of the Year ...*

So, I was in. In spite of everything that had happened so far, I was going to the ball. Well, I was going to the Hairdresser Ball anyway. I was still excluded from the

Love Ball. There were no texts from Tony. No calls or emails. I'd managed to avoid him at school by retreating to my old haunt – the school library – at lunchtimes. Miss Frame my only favourite teacher was always there too; stamping the books and alphabetising and being self-controlled and self-contained and just, well, *cool* for a teacher.

I'd found myself wanting to copy one of her hairstyles; she favoured the fifties and she had this neat little fringe and then a high pony. She teamed it with a little-girl hairslide at the side. It was cute.

'I get them online,' Miss Frame had said to me that Friday. She must have sensed me staring at it. 'TeddyGirlStyle.com.'

'Great,' I said. 'I'll try it.'

'I hear you have a job in a salon these days,' said Miss Frame. She smiled at me. She was like a little china doll, her features all neat – the little red heart-shaped buttons on her blouse so shiny.

'I do,' I said.

'Hard work?'

'You could say . . .'

'Well, good for you,' said Miss Frame. 'You have

determination, Sadie. It's really . . .' She paused very deliberately. I watched the way she breathed – the way she put her hand on her chest – the way the little red heart-shaped buttons went up and down. 'It's really – I think it's commendable to have found something you want to do and to go for it,' Miss Frame continued. 'It takes a lot of adults years to find their way to whatever it is they want to work at. Some of them never find it.'

I smiled. 'I've always, always wanted to do hairdressing.'

'And you're doing it!' said Miss Frame. 'Hard work though. All that standing up . . . and that salon you're in – I'll bet it's busy.'

It was.

In fact we were packed to the tracklights that Saturday. There were four clients waiting for Misha. Unlike Dariusz, she didn't exactly have a booking system. Hers was more like: *You can come in, but you have to get in line*. Hence the queue.

Dariusz had a spiral perm on the go and extensions waiting. I had a full head of low-lights followed by a re-style, which Dariusz was going to do, but I was invited to observe. On top of that I had to unblock the sinks,

186

make the coffees, meet and greet. And I had to sweep. It was a tall order, but I was determined to rise to the challenge of being in three places at once. Now I was getting everywhere through sheer determination – making myself indispensable. I wanted Dariusz Zengelis to say, 'What would I do without Sadie Nathanson? What did I do before I had Sadie Nathanson?'

I raced, broom in hand, around the shop floor in between cuts. I ran to the sinks and pulled out the hairs, swilling them around with a J Cloth in between washes.

Then on to the low-lights.

'Brrrrush,' I muttered under my breath, and with poise and elegance I greeted the client, holding my head erect and gliding across the floor.

Dariusz did the consult with the client, Elodie B. I'd seen her around. Enrico had said she was cool when we were in his car once. Once when I was happy because I had everything going on – the boyfriend, the career . . .

'What face-shape are we looking at here, Sadie?' said Dariusz pulling my attention back into the salon.

'Oval,' I said, almost without thinking. Oval was a hairdresser's dream. Heart-shaped meant side-swept bangs. Round faces suited long waves but not curls, and long faces suited curls but not long waves.

I had begun to realise that hairdressing wasn't just about channelling hair. There were rules too, and Dariusz was a stickler for making me practise them.

Elodie B wanted low-lights and so each little packet of foil was folded and creased to perfection. The colour was one of the more exciting shades from the Clairvoyant range and the client was classy too, and hell – you know what? That Saturday at Stylee Stylee, Roman Road I was starting to enjoy myself for the first time in what felt like forever. I wasn't checking my phone every half-hour for Tony's texts, and Billy had stopped leaving me messages full of sighs. I could almost pretend that Tony had never existed and that Billy wasn't going to leave Rock Dove and last Saturday night hadn't ever happened. Even Aunt Lilah's salon seemed light years away and, most important of all, didn't I have a new sister with good hair who wanted to be my friend? Running around Stylee Stylee was what I'd always dreamed of when I chose this profession. Interesting clients and a boss I could learn from. It was all working out for me after all. I was making it happen all on my own. I was showing everyone.

And then I looked up and Tony was there. *Oh God! Tony!* My heart leaped in my chest. Finally he'd come to apologise – and I would forgive him. I just knew it. We'd been crazy to break up over our first argument. I waited for him to smile at me, nod his head – something Tony-ish. But he didn't. He was standing by the door, signalling to me. Showing me his watch – like one o'clock suddenly meant I could leave a queue of clients, an unblocked sink and a pile of unswept hair and just go for my lunch break. Like that would have gone down well with Mr Psycho Boss.

But I couldn't leave Tony standing there either. Dariusz would get wind of it. He'd get all uncomfortable. He might also think that if Tony was there then Enrico might be around. There was a possibility that he'd get all jumpy and over-excited. It was a mess. I needed to deal with the situation pronto.

With my client safely under the lights, I went to the door. I raised my eyebrows at Tony questioningly.

He said nothing. He stared at the ground. He didn't apologise. His stance was guarded. Clearly the break-up was still on.

Well, two could play at that game.

'What?' I said. 'What d'you want?'

'To talk to you,' said Tony.

I stiffened. I remembered his last words to me. *You don't know what it's like to have a regular family.* I looked at him. He didn't look sorry. He plainly hadn't come here to apologise. He'd come here 'to talk' – to justify his actions. To tell me once again that he hadn't been ready to share the information about Enrico and Dariusz and that I'd never understand this, being that I wasn't actually normal.

And then I wondered whether Billy had told him about Interpol – about leaving the band – and it occurred to me that maybe I wasn't ready to share that information either. So he might as well just leave because the whole thing was still a mess.

In another life I would have told him about getting through to the heats. We would have celebrated. We would have tried to find a corner to make out in. We would have been interrupted. But we weren't in another life. We were stuck firmly in this one, which seemed to consist of lies and withholding from one another – the very opposite of TLC in my book.

'From where I'm stood I think we've got nothing to talk about,' I said.

Tony looked down. He wasn't nodding. He looked less than positive. A lot less.

Then Dariusz emerged behind me.

'I don't pay you to chat up your boyfriend, Sadie. Floors and sinks! Floors and sinks!'

That was all it took. I turned on my heel and headed back into the salon. I was Sadie Nathanson: Hairdressing Machine. I wasn't a useless Saturday numpty who bitched at her boyfriend on the doorstep, flossed her teeth with the clients' stray hair and sneaked copies of *Heat* up her sleeve at the end of the day.

While I unblocked the sink I could see Tony waving at Aimée Price in Cissor's Palace – Unisex Hairdresser, or was Aimée Price waving at him? I mean, how did Tony even know Aimée Price? He'd only heard of her because I'd mentioned how annoying she was. I saw Aimée come to the door of Misty's domain. I tried not to care. I saw Aimée opening the door and ushering him in. They stood for some time by the window. Aimée was gesturing at Dariusz's salon. They were openly pointing at me.

'Hair, Sadie!' said Dariusz in my ear, 'Pile of . . .'

I grabbed the broom and went on my rounds, resolving once again to do better. To block out the distractions. But a half-hour later the distraction was coming my way. Aimée Price crashing through the door, waving like royalty to everyone. Like she was a celebrity . . . like she was . . .

'Sadie!' She leaned over the sinks and stage whispered into my face. 'Sadie.'

'Hi,' I said with as little expression as possible. I could feel Dariusz boring his pits of doom our way.

'All right, Dariusz!' Aimée called out before he could moan about her distracting me. Then she turned back to me. 'You get through? Heats yeah? Competition here we come? Hmm?'

I nodded.

'You look thrilled!'

'I am,' I said flatly.

'Y'know, nobody else made it from our class – just me and you . . .'

How did she know this? How did Aimée Price know this stuff? We only just got our letters. She must've called everyone in the class. But before I could ask, she was off on another tack.

'I just had your break-up in my shop,' she said.

'Yeah?' I said, like I hadn't noticed. Like I didn't care.

'Well, I think he's your break-up . . . But anyhow – I wanted to check – is he your ex? Cos I invited him to a party tonight that my friend Felicia is having and I didn't want to, y'know, invite him if he's still your fella and all that. Know what I'm saying?'

'S'fine,' I mumbled. I managed to say it like I meant it was all fine. After all, I totally deserved everything she'd just dished out. I deserved it for the way I told her about Dariusz. I deserved it for being a total bitch. But God, that didn't stop me from being mad as hell with her too.

'Y'know,' said Aimée, 'you're my friend here and all that. But Felicia's short on fellas for the party so that's why I invited Tony, but I wanted to check with you first. I mean there's nothing in it. I don't like . . . y'know . . .'

'Aimée,' I said. 'I have a client under the lights and a boss breathing down my neck. You can invite Tony. You don't need to ask my permission. We're all grown-ups here. Well, some of us are.'

I couldn't help myself. I just couldn't. She pushed all my buttons. In a very bad way.

193

Aimée Price raised her eyebrows at me. She totally got it. 'OK, Miss Thing – you have made yourself understood. Loud and Clear. Licken Chicken,' she said.

I went back to unblocking the sinks. When I looked up she was gone. *Poof.*

I looked over at Dariusz doing the spiral perm. He rolled it and sprayed it, then added some serum to the ends. He was fast. He was furious.

He was sniffing the air.

'What the hell is that smell?'

I looked over at the client I'd been looking after earlier. Yes, the smell was Elodie B. Her hair was toasting fiercely under the lights. Little wisps of smoke climbed towards the ceiling. I took a flying leap towards the thermostat, but Dariusz got there before me. With one flick of his wrist he turned it to zero. He lifted the lights from Elodie B and smiled at her.

'No damage done!' he breezed. 'Misha!' he yelled. 'Finish up here, darling.'

Misha swung around. She had three clients waiting. She was in the middle of a fusion situation. Then she saw the look on Dariusz's face. She put down the comb and went straight over to Elodie B.

'Sadie,' said Dariusz very quietly, 'can you just come with me?'

Dariusz took me to the store cupboard where we hung our housecoats. And then he fired my ass.

'You put the thermostat on its highest setting. We never ever do that. You were distracted. You lost concentration. You are a loose cannon.'

That phrase again. *Loose cannon*.

'I . . . I was sure I . . .'

'Tabard, please!' he said.

I removed my apron and scissors and handed them over. My tools. My trophies.

'Now leave, please,' said Dariusz, 'and don't come back.'

I breathed in. I thought 'brrrrush'.

And then I was gone.

Darius closed the door behind me and once again my life was over.

22

Family is Family

The trainee hairdresser (or barber) should learn from their mistakes. If the attitude of the mentor remains nurturing and encouraging then the trainee stands a much better chance of learning from and not repeating the mistake.

Guideline 22: Thames Gateway Junior Apprentice Hairdresser (or Barber) of the Year Award

'Actually, I think I made a mistake,' said Aunt Lilah, and she stared hard at me over the glasses she wears for trimming around people's ears or for reading the instructions on the colour packs. She raised her pencilled-on eyebrows.

'How d'you mean?' I said.

I don't think I had ever heard Aunt Lilah mention a mistake, in connection with herself and something she might have made, before. It sort of shocked me.

'Mrs Nellist came to see me,' she said. 'About a week after . . . y'know.'

'A week after you fired me?'

'Ye-es,' she said. I could have sworn that her cheeks went pinker under the layer of foundation that looked as if it had been applied with a trowel.

We were standing in her salon and she was washing the sinks. Tiffany had gone and enrolled herself two afternoons a week on a beautician course, which meant that Aunt Lilah was having to cover on her own. She was desperate. I was desperate. I was aware that desperation was our common ground here – the root of this conversation.

I was fairly sure that Aunt Lilah didn't really think she'd made a mistake about firing me.

'Mrs Nellist loved her hair, as it turns out,' said Aunt Lilah, scrubbing hard at a stray splash of Rose Madder that had speckled the work top.

'I know,' I said.

'You know?' That look over the glasses again.

'I ran into her,' I said. 'couple of days after you fired me. She couldn't stop talking about it. I never thought she would come and tell you though.'

'Why didn't *you* come in and tell me?' said Aunt Lilah.

'Well, there didn't seem to be much point. You didn't fire me over whether Mrs Nellist liked her hair or not, did you. It was about my attitude. Whether Mrs Nellist liked her hair wasn't really relevant to you, was it?'

I should be a lawyer. Really, I'm so wasted on hairdressing.

'Well the point is, I think that maybe I was a bit hasty,' said Aunt Lilah. 'And I think your man on Roman Road has been a bit hasty as well, if you ask me. Running your own salon is not easy – you'll find out one day. Lots of pressure. You can't afford for things to go wrong.'

'So you don't think it might be a pattern then?' I said. 'You don't think I'm a *loose cannon* who can't take instruction, doesn't concentrate, makes mistakes?'

Small wisps of self-doubt were surrounding me like the wisps of smoke that had surrounded Elodie B, the client I had almost fried the day before.

'We all make mistakes,' said Aunt Lilah. 'That's how we learn. But I think you were right about Mrs Nellist.

I think she did want a change. She loved her hair. You got it right. You took a risk, and you're very young to be taking risks, but on this occasion I'll admit that it paid off. You have a good instinct for hair, Sadie.'

'Thank you,' I said. And I meant it.

And really it was so good to hear. Affirmation. *From Aunt Lilah*. It was a miracle. Maybe she actually meant it.

'At the end of the day family is family,' said Aunt Lilah, like we were on *Eastenders*.

Thank you, Mrs Nellist. And thank you, Tiffany, for doing the beautician course. I tried to imagine Tiffany in a white coat, waxing upper lips. Was it responsible to employ someone who forgot to pay their brain bill most of the time, and then let them loose on beings with nerve endings? Maybe there was a market for coral polyp beauticians, or even sponge doctors – any entity without a central nerve chord I was sure even Tiffany could handle.

'Sadie – I'm willing to give you another chance,' said Aunt Lilah, 'because I think you have genuine talent. But you have to promise me that you *will* do the donkey work and you *will* pay attention . . .'

I nodded like my head was going to fall off.

'. . . and you won't go off and do your own thing without consulting me first of all?'

She wanted me to be her salon bitch, and you know what? I was willing to do it. I would do practically anything she asked me to right then. Because if I didn't I'd have to kiss goodbye to everything I'd been working towards since, like, forever.

'Of course I will, Aunty,' I said.

Aunt Lilah came out from behind the sink and held out her arms to me. Being hugged by Aunt Lilah was like being hugged by a make-up counter. For several moments a miasma of powder, glitter and perfume descended on me. Like the Iceland Ash Cloud by Max Factor. In spite of the fact that I knew there would be lipstick on my cheek and maybe on my clothes, and the smell of products would linger forever, I felt moved by the hug. Even if it was because Aunty was so desperate to replace Tiffany, at least it *felt* like a kindness. Kindness was something I definitely needed right now. Wasn't I still smarting from being kicked out of Dariusz's salon?

I had played the scene over and over in my head. How I'd put Elodie B under the lights, set the thermostat to medium, set the timer and then gone to speak to Tony. I could almost *see* the thermostat at medium. I was so sure I'd set it right. After all, it was just basic hairdresser training.

But I had been distracted by so much that day. I'd made a mistake. I must have made a mistake. Now I couldn't afford to make another one. Even in Aunt Lilah's salon I couldn't. Everything would be over for me if I did. I'd have to consider becoming a nuclear physicist instead.

'So, what d'you say?' said Aunt Lilah. She was concentrating hard on the sinks. She was trying not to come over too Needy Gonzales. 'Two afternoons a week – straight from school you come in here and deal with whatever's going: front desk, sinks, washing heads, colours, coffees, sweeping up. If there's time you get to watch me cut.'

Gee. Thanks for that. I get to watch you take a centimetre off all over. Maybe even a fringe tidy-up. 'I'll do it.' I said.

She smiled. 'Good, that's settled then.' She looked relieved. 'Now, come and bleach these sinks for me, would you?'

Back on track again. For the second time in a month I had a new job.

23

Yank My Roots

Due to the nature of the job, the hairdresser (or barber) will need to be very physical with the client. Gentleness but firmness is the aim in cutting, washing and all techniques. A decisive stroke is very important, but so is sensitivity to the client's physical feelings.

Guideline 23: Thames Gateway Junior Apprentice Hairdresser (or Barber) of the Year Award

'It was a crazy party,' said Aimée Price.

Once again Florence had paired us up and now she was attacking me with the straightening irons. Pulling down from the roots. Hard. Hard. Hard. I screwed up my eyes. I would remember not to pull like this – it hurt like hell. But I wouldn't tell Aimée. Wait till a customer yelled out – then she might realise.

'You should've been there!' she went on.

'Well, I wasn't actually invited,' I said. *Duh-uh*.

'Your boyf – your *ex*-boyf enjoyed plenty,' said Aimée. She was sporting ten different coloured acrylics on her fingers. Nine junk nails with diamante inserts. One with an actual chain running through it. There was no way you could match your outfit to that combo, so Aimée Price was wearing black again. It suited her. She looked good. I should have told her so, but I kept it to myself.

'Tony sang "Happy Birthday",' Aimée went on, 'and y'know Felicia's a pretty good singer too, so she joined in and they were great together.' She looked sideways at me. 'Just singing together – OK?'

Ouch. It hurt, and Aimée wasn't even pulling my hair that time. It was the thought of Tony and Felicia. *Must not care must not care* . . . I repeated my mantra silently.

'I don't particularly care what they were doing together, Aimée,' I said. 'Tony Cruz is not my *boyf* any more. He is a free agent. He can do as he likes – with whoever he likes.'

'OK,' said Aimée and she yanked my roots again. Some future client would slap her for less. Soon and hard, hopefully.

'Your cousin was there too, y'know,' Aimée carried

on. 'Well he was there for a bit. He came with Tony and then they seemed to get into some kind of a row. Tony said it was about the band – y'know, that Rock Bird thing they play in. Not my kinda music, but Felicia likes it.'

Felicia likes it. Likes it or him? Likes it or Tony Cruz? I wasn't saying a word.

'So they had this row and your cousin went off pretty early. He looked upset. So did Tony –I don't know if it was about you, but whatever – it looked like it might be serious.'

The band. Billy had told Tony he was leaving the band.

'Tony was upset, but luckily Felicia managed to cheer him up . . .'

'OUCH!' I yelled at the top of my voice. I couldn't listen to another word. I didn't want to hear another minute of how Felicia cheered up Tony.

'Jeez!' said Aimée. 'What the HELL's up with you all of a sudden?'

I stood up and removed the straightening irons from her grasp. 'You are pulling my hair way too hard! IT HURTS – THAT'S WHY I'M YELLING!'

'Girls! Girls! Girls!' said Florence, tearing over from the other side of the room.

Aimée Price and I were facing each other. Narrowed eyes. Chins out. Hands on hips. Faces full of rage. I guess Florence was worried there was about to be a fight because I was, after all, holding a pair of heated straightening irons. I put them down.

'It's fine,' I said to Florence. 'She's just pulling too hard and I'm not feeling well. I'm going to go home if you don't mind.'

I turned to find my bag and coat. My eyes misted over, which was getting to be a habit and I didn't like it one bit.

'OK,' said Florence, 'I will give you a permission slip but I really don't like the yelling, Sadie – or Aimée. This is supposed to be a teaching room. That noise was loud and it was vulgar. You are the students in this college who have qualified for a major competition – you should be behaving like professionals.'

On my way home I texted Billy;

> **SD: Hv u told Tony?**
> **Billy: Bout wot?**
> **SD: U know. Band. Hv u?**

Billy: Yes
SD: How did he take it?

My phone rang.

'Badly,' said Billy. 'He took it really badly.'

He sighed into the phone. If Marie was an Olympic-standard chatter, my cousin Billy could go for gold in sighing. There were so many different sighs in so many combinations. This sigh was the saddest of them all though. It was kind of out through his nose, but with an extra groaning dimension in the background. I couldn't remember when the sighing thing had started exactly, but it seemed to have been with us way too long.

'Why?' I said. 'What did he say? What happened?'

'Well,' said Billy, 'we were at this party – y'know that girl from the Catholic school? Year 11, with the voice and the . . .'

'And the chest?' I said. 'Felicia?'

Boys were all the same. Even boys I was related to, it seemed.

'That's it. Felicia. Friend of whatsername with the matching whatsits.'

'Aimée Price.'

207

'That's it. Well, anyway, we were at Felicia's party and Tony sang "Happy Birthday" and she joined in – Felicia – and actually she has a pretty good voice . . .'

Good voice, or nice mouth with a large pair of lungs attached? I didn't care for Felicia's voice one bit. I needed to know what had happened at her party between Billy and Tony though.

'So anyway, they sang and then Tony came up to me and said we should think about having a female singer in the band maybe and how did I feel about it and all. And I said I thought it was fine and that it wasn't really down to me any more because I needed to tell him something.'

Subtle. Not.

Billy continued. 'And so Tony goes, "Don't tell me you're leaving the band?" and I said, "Yes, as a matter of fact I am leaving the band, but only because somebody else has asked me to play in their band."'

Oh God.

'And Tony said that only made it worse, that it wasn't like I was giving up because I had too much study to do for preparing for uni and all that but because I'd found something better and he said he couldn't really speak to me because he was so angry, and then he asked me if you knew.'

Oh. Dear. God.

'And what did you say?' I asked. I asked it very hesitantly because truthfully I didn't like where this was going one bit.

'I said yes, because you did, but I said you'd only just found out.'

Not good. Really not good.

'And what did Tony say when you said I knew?'

Another sigh. Then silence.

'Billy . . . what did Tony say?'

'Well, he didn't say much. In fact, he never said anything. He just looked pissed-off and, yeah, deflated – let-down and every other thing I knew he would be. I feel really, really bad about it, but, y'know, my heart hasn't been in it for a while now and I have tried to tell him for ages and –'

'It's OK, Billy,' I interrupted him. 'You don't have to justify any of this to me at all. You have to do your thing and Tony will be upset about it, and then Felicia will sing and then they'll probably become an item and maybe they'll get married and he'll forget all about both of us . . .'

'What are you talking about?' said Billy. 'Tony is mad about you. He's not going to forget about you and go out with Felicia. You are what he cares about most.'

That's what Billy said. And when I finished the call and I got off the bus by the Fish House and went up the steps to my flat and sat in my room and looked out of the window over at the park – well, that was all I could think about.

Tony is mad about you.

He's not going to forget about you.

Exactly what kind of a fool was I to let that go?

24

And Another Friday Night Family Tea

Making a brand new client feel welcome in the salon should be a priority for the trainee hairdresser (or barber). Meeting and greeting, discussing requirements and booking in should be done in a friendly but professional manner.

Guideline 24: Thames Gateway Junior Apprentice Hairdresser (or Barber) of the Year Award

Why did I allow members of my family to meet other members of my family? Friday night tea and I'd invited Marie. Yes, so soon. What was wrong with me?

Of course, I had warned her. I'd warned her about the indigestion tablets and the food combinations, and that Great Aunty Rita wouldn't understand who she was or would pretend not to, and about Mum's tendency to get very sentimental, and about Aunt Lilah and Uncle

Zé and about Billy's sighing and general geekiness.

But Marie was not to be put off. She was totally Game On.

'I love big families!' she said, a huge smile covering her face in what I now recognised as her default expression. Marie was continuously upbeat. We were on our way over to Aunt Lilah's from my flat and she was skipping along the pavement like a little girl. Although I liked her and thought her hair was neat, Marie's energy was making me feel . . . jaded or tired or something.

'I always wanted a big family,' Marie continued. 'There was only ever me and Mum and Dad and that was it: Christmas, New Year, birthdays, holidays – just the three of us. It was fine, but I was always fascinated by my friends' Christmases, with all those presents and dinners and relatives . . .'

'Yeah,' I said. 'Well, big families are fine and all, but they can be a bit, y'know . . .' I watched Marie skipping from paving stone to paving stone – not touching the cracks. 'A bit tiring . . .'

The word was definitely 'tiring'.

And when it came to my family specifically, the words were: Tiring. Annoying. Homicide-inducing.

*

'She's who?' said Great Aunty Rita, moving her chair back from the loaded dinner table to get a better look at Marie.

'Marie is my half-sister, Aunty,' I said again.

Aunty Rita looked blank.

'Remember Abe?' I tried again.

'Who?'

'Abe's our father, Aunty Rita!' shrieked Marie, like Aunty Rita was deaf, senile and also an infant. 'Sadie and I share a father!'

Aunty Rita stared back at Marie. Her eyes flicked up and down disapprovingly.

'I wouldn't put it past him,' she said darkly.

Sometimes I thought that Great Aunty Rita understood everything perfectly well. She just wanted to make sure we understood that she understood.

'Well, it is just lovely to meet you,' said Mum, gripping Marie's hand and pulling up a chair for her, a tear beginning to form in the corner of her eye. 'And I can see Abe there, y'know,' she peered into Marie's face. 'In the way that I can with Sadie. It's subtle, but there is a similarity.'

There was in truth absolutely no similarity. Apart from the hands. I had studied us. You would never have picked us out as being related.

'Well, I can't see any similarity, sis,' said Aunt Lilah, telling it how it was. And for once I agreed with her.

'You're lovely, dear,' said Aunt Lilah, which of course implied that I wasn't. 'I like the way you do your hair – look at the way she does her hair, Sadie.' Like I hadn't noticed the way Marie did her hair.

'It's great! We should suggest it in the salon.' I forced a smile. After all, hadn't Aunt Lilah just given me my job back?

'You could model!' said Aunt Lilah, seating herself on the other side of Marie, who was now giggling and mock-protesting.

'She could, though, couldn't she model, Billy?' insisted Aunt Lilah.

'Huh?' said Billy. There was an odd expression on Billy's face that I'd never really seen before. Well, maybe once before. A very long time ago, involving an ex-best friend of mine whose photo Billy became rather attached to.

'She looks like . . . oh, who is it?' Aunt Lilah was off on one of her tangents. 'What was her name? Y'know – that model. The one with the teeth.'

I shrugged at Marie and raised my eyebrows. I was trying to convey the message to just ignore my aunt because she's highly irritating and she mostly talks total rubbish.

To give Aunt Lilah her due, she had succeeded in almost silencing Marie. Aunt Lilah and Marie reminded me of something we'd learned in physics about two forces of equal magnitude cancelling each other out. At the moment Aunt Lilah was winning though.

'She was on that programme about serial killers,' Aunt Lilah continued, 'wasn't she, Zé?'

'What's that, dear?' said Uncle Zé from the kitchen.

Uncle Zé was frying up the *tsitsaron* (bits of pork) to go with the pork.

'Marie – she looks like that actress, the one with the teeth.'

'Julia Roberts,' said Uncle Zé.

Obviously he thought Marie was gorgeous too. It was starting to get on my nerves the way everyone was fawning over my half-sister.

'Not Julia Roberts.' Aunt Lilah wasn't letting it drop. 'The one in the serial killers programme – you do know, Zé. She used to model.'

Uncle Zé said nothing. He put the plate of *tsitsaron* on the table. Next to the potato *latkes* and fried *matzo* balls.

Aunt Lilah sat back in her chair and helped herself to a pickled cucumber. She had finally fizzled out.

'Well you're very welcome anyway,' said Mum. 'It's great to have you with us this evening.'

'It's *Shabbus*,' said Great Aunty Rita to Marie by way of explanation. 'Do you do Friday nights at home or are you out at the synagogue?'

Marie looked blank. She shook her head at Aunty Rita, who smiled secretly to herself. She really was a wicked old woman.

'*Shabbus* is the Jewish Sabbath,' I explained.

'Oh,' said Marie. She still looked confused.

Later, as Mum and I drove Marie over to Charing Cross station so that she could catch her train back down to Canterbury and to her mother who wasn't able to acknowledge us just yet, Marie said, 'It's really odd, Sadie, but I always had the impression that Jews don't eat pork. I don't know why I always thought that.'

'Ahh, but we're very special Jews,' I said. 'We have a Filipino twist.'

'Yes,' said Marie, 'so you do . . . And now we're related I guess I do too, sort of!'

She was right. And maybe I might get to be part of her quirky little tribe too, when the time was right. You don't get to pick your family, do you. That's what people say (and some people say that your family are God's gift to you) and well – actually, that's not strictly true. You don't get to choose your first family – the one you're born into – but you do mostly get to choose your next family: your husband/ your boyfriend/ the community you move to/ your friends/ whatever.

Mum chose carefully. She chose Abe, and she chose to keep Aunt Lilah and Uncle Zé close by. But then someone else chose Abe too – and quite possibly someone else and someone else. And Mum *didn't* get to choose who else chose Abe, so then it all got a bit random and who knew how many half-Abe replicants with weird shaky hands there were out there?

But so far it was random in a rather wonderful way. I mean, Marie was great. She was a little upbeat for me, and she had an awful lot of energy, but I guess I'd just got lucky with something important in my life, even if everything else had imploded.

Later, I sat upstairs in my bedroom and looked out over at the street lamps in the park.

That park was where Tony and I had gone when we first got together. The children's playground, the see-saw where I'd nearly fatally wounded him.

Tony is mad about you.

He's not going to forget about you.

And try as I might, I hadn't forgotten about him either.

25

Yet Another Apology, Sort of

The trainee hairdresser (or barber) should understand early on that they have chosen a trade that is physically demanding as well as creatively challenging. Entrants to the competition will be expected to spend up to eight hours a day on their feet during their apprenticeship.

Guideline 25: Thames Gateway Junior Apprentice Hairdresser (or Barber) of the Year Award

So I was sweeping the shop from left to right facing the back door, so that the hair went downhill and when the wind blew it didn't go all over the shop, when Dariusz Zengelis walked in.

It had been a frantic afternoon – only my third shift at Delilah's since Aunty gave me back my job, and I don't mind telling you that I was working my buns to the bone. Aunty had made Uncle Zé do a leaflet drop, giving 25 per cent off all treatments, and the place had become so busy that I was actually starting to think I'd under-estimated Tiffany. The way she shuffled around the place, the way she talked so slowly, the way she repeated everything Aunt Lilah said – perhaps she was masking a real talent at making everything look relaxed and easy, because she did and I didn't.

I was completely hyper-manic. When I wasn't mixing colour I was meeting and greeting – talking nineteen to the dozen, taking coats, putting on gowns, ripping them off again, making coffee like some demented dervish and stirring two cups at once, booking appointments with a teaspoon tucked behind my ear – doing highlights, low-lights, perms under driers, washing heads, drying heads, wiping down surfaces, unblocking sinks and sweeping the shop from left to right, and all with the word 'brrrrush' in my head. You get the picture. I wondered whether it might be a good idea to get rollerblades because I spent so much time running from one end of the shop to the other. Aunty was as busy as Dariusz now, even if the average age of her clients was twice the age of his.

'You are doing a good job, my girl,' said Aunt Lilah. 'You are doing fine.'

220

Whatever it was – Tiffany's absence, my desperation, the knock-backs of the last few weeks, Dariusz Zengelis's insistence that I repeat every hairdressing technique fifty times to get it right, Aimée Price being picked out for back-combing, maybe even the row with Tony – now it felt like it was all coming together for me at Delilah's.

The last thing I needed was Dariusz Zengelis rocking up to remind me how useless I was.

'I have made a mistake,' said Dariusz.

I gripped my broom and stared at him. What was that? Calm. *Calm. Very calm. Stay very calm. Dignity. Grace. Brrrrush.*

He stood in front of the pile of hair I was about to sweep. 'I'm sweeping that,' I said pointlessly.

I waved the broom a bit, expecting him to budge. I was trying to be normal. Like I didn't care less. He didn't budge.

I walked around him and continued sweeping. For once *I* was busy and he was disturbing *me*. Why was Aunt Lilah's salon any less important than his? How come it was acceptable for him to interrupt my work in her salon, but no one was allowed to interrupt me in his?

'Tell me, who is minding my shop?' Dariusz asked me.

'Your new trainee, I expect,' I said – I was being bold. 'Your new fierce and fabulous trainee?'

'Wrong,' he said. 'I don't have a new trainee. There is no one in my shop but me this afternoon, and I have had to close my shop while I come here to tell you that I have made a mistake,'

He'd said it again.

'I made a mistake. I owe you an apology.' Dariusz drew back his lips and gripped his front teeth together, like it was physically painful to squeeze out the words. 'I have never closed my shop before. I am here because this is serious.'

I was fairly sure that Dariusz had picked this moment because he had a break between clients. I just couldn't quite see him walking out in the middle of an appointment, somehow. Still. It was kind of awesome that he was bothering to tell me any of this.

'So you've finally realised that I wasn't so useless after all?' I said, scarcely believing the exchange we were having.

'No, it's not that,' said Dariusz.

Of course it wasn't that – what idiot thought it was?

'I have found out,' Dariusz continued, 'that our friend from over the road tampered with the thermostat on my lights.'

'Huh?'

It was hard to take in what Dariusz was saying.

He was sorry.

He had made a mistake.

And finally, it wasn't me that had turned up the heat to maximum on his precious lights.

I had played and replayed that scene over and over in my head. I seat Elodie B. I pull down the lights with one hand and with my free hand I turn the dial halfway. HALFWAY. It was always halfway. I would never just keep on and on turning to max.

'Firstly,' continued Dariusz, 'Elodie told me, "Dariusz I think you make a mistake – it was that other girl." I said, "What other girl? There is only Sadie." She kept insisting, "It's that other girl – the one with the nails." And secondly – your ex, Tony, comes in, and then he made Aimée come in too.'

Aimée? It was Aimée Price.

'It was Aimée Price?' I said.

'She swore it was just a joke when she told Tony about it,' Dariusz continued. 'But Tony had heard you'd been fired — I think from Enrico. So Tony was furious and he told Aimée it was no laughing matter. He said that she had to come in and tell me herself. Even Enrico came to see me. By that point I was like, "All right, all right, I understand, it wasn't Sadie. I *comprende, señor*. I *kapeesh* you, all right?"'

I stared at him. I didn't know what to say. I was lost in space.

'I mean, I have to work sometime without all these interruptions. I have clients. I have customers. I have a fabulous ordering system your cousin set up for me . . .'

'But I have a job now,' I interrupted him. 'Here.' I stared around Delilah's. It was the truth. I couldn't just bail now and go back.

My gesture took in the whole of Aunt Lilah's drab little salon. The unfashionable chairs, the streaking caps, the old-fashioned sinks, the photos of Jenifer Aniston in her 'Rachel' phase. Dariusz stared around the salon too, nodding his head as if to say, 'Yeah — this is about where I thought you might end up, Sadie Nathanson.'

'Well, that was quick. You sure got another job

quick,' was what Dariusz actually said. His face looked almost disappointed. His shrinkled neck sagged even further into his too-tight T-shirt.

'I had to take this job,' I said. 'I'm in this competition in like three weeks' time. I needed a position.'

'Well, hell, you can have two positions!' said Dariusz. 'What days you do here?'

'Monday afternoon and Wednesday late night. We do free tea, coffee and biscuits for that. We're completely packed with little old ladies in hairnets who just come for the custard creams. I spend the whole evening boiling the kettle.'

'So you do Saturday for me!' said Dariusz.

So that would be Monday to Friday school and college, Monday and Wednesday after school Aunt Lilah's, and Saturday Dariusz. And Sunday? How about Sunday? Maybe I could take a tap-dancing class on a Sunday.

'Sure . . .' I said, uncertainly.

'Look,' said Dariusz, 'you have two or three weeks left until the competition. Get as much experience and practice as you can, and then afterwards you can decide where you'd like to work. OK?'

I didn't say anything. It was so odd to go from having been fired from two jobs to being begged by both the salon owners to come back.

'It's my final offer,' said Dariusz. 'Think about it. And maybe I'll see you on Saturday.'

I leaned on my broom. I was thinking about it. I was considering whether or not it would be the sensible thing to do; considering whether or not Dariusz Zengelis was worthy of my assistance.

But I knew for a fact that wild horses wouldn't keep me from Stylee Stylee, Roman Road on Saturday morning.

'I'll be there,' I said.

26

Yet another apology, a real one this time

The trainee hairdresser (or barber) will benefit from some intelligent and honest feedback from the mentor. If this is not forthcoming during salon hours, it would be wise to seek this out of hours.

Guideline 26: Thames Gateway Junior Apprentice Hairdresser (or Barber) of the Year Award

I had two jobs and I was back in the race. The first person I wanted to call to tell him my news was Tony. But I couldn't.

Tony Cruz was the big missing piece from my puzzle, and when I took five seconds out of my Incredibly Important and Busy Schedule to think about it, I knew I had to try to put that right. So I went to see him.

'I made a terrible mistake,' I said as soon as he opened the front door.

'Huh?' said Tony.

'Look, I owe you an apology.'

There had been a lot of apologising lately. There had been a lot of mistakes made. Aunt Lilah. Dariusz.

And now me, Sadie Nathanson, apologising to Tony Cruz, who she wouldn't listen to and who she'd lied to – or rather withheld vital information from – but who she really, really loved.

'You'd better come in,' said Tony. His voice was a flat monotone. There was no animation. He turned mechanically and went inside.

I followed him in. I noticed how his shoulders drooped. There was no nodding or smiling. His back view was frankly depressing. His jeans were pulled low down so you could see the top of his pants, and there was a label sticking out that I couldn't help noticing and which said 'Wash Hot, Age 11'. I could just picture the epic pile of laundry in the corner of his bedroom. It had been two weeks since our argument and he was down to the really ancient pants. This was worse than I'd feared.

It was a weekday and so there was nobody else in Tony's house. I'd checked the music lab that lunchtime and Billy confirmed that Tony hadn't shown up at school. So I was missing double business studies to stick my neck out and see that he was OK and to ask him if we could stop being mad at one another and start being boyfriend and girlfriend again.

There was just no contest between business studies and Tony Cruz, even with his current depressing back view and really ancient pants.

We stood at opposite ends of the lounge like we needed this giant space in between us in order to have a conversation. It was a cloudy day and there were no lights on in the room – just the gloom beyond the patio doors – so I could barely see his face.

'You should've told me about Enrico,' I said. 'But I should've got over it and I'm really, really sorry.' I was nodding and shaking my head like I was mimicking his habitual gestures – trying to get some positivity going.

Through the dim light I could see Tony blinking and beginning to nod too, which was kind of reassuring.

'And you should've tried to see things from my point of view as well,' he said. 'And you should've talked to me when I came to the salon, and you should've told me about Billy.'

His list of 'should'ves' was longer than mine. There was no doubt about it. He was the more-injured party and he required some kind of an explanation. So I gave him one.

'I fully admit that I was mad and behaving like a loon recently,' I said. 'But you have no idea about all this other stuff that's been going on for me. I have, like, a new sister – Marie – who's appeared out of the blue, and I've had all the preparation for the competition, which has just been driving me crazy. And then Aimée pulling that stunt and Dariusz firing me and Aunt Lilah firing me and them both begging me to come back so that now I have two jobs. And my . . . *thing* – the thing that I do best in the whole world, my ability to do hair – well, my confidence in that has been shot to pieces twice, and then resurrected twice! And I have to say "brrrrush" and perform – just like magic. It's mental. It's bonkers. And I am really really sorry about all of it. And I'm sorry I got mad at you of all people . . .'

Tony turned around at that point, like he couldn't listen to me any longer. He turned and faced the patio doors and stared up into the sky like he was looking for the answer to all of this, and as he did so I could see the label that said 'Wash Hot, Age 11' and it made me feel so tender towards him that I could hardly breathe. Then he spoke.

'You had to choose between your loyalty to Billy and your loyalty to me,' he said, 'and I know what that's like and I get it and I don't hate you for it. But you have to understand that I wanted to respect *my* brother's privacy, and I can see that it might've made you feel insecure and –'

I walked over to him and put my finger on his lips.

'Shhhh . . .' I said. 'None of it matters now. All that matters is that we belong together and we should be together.'

He took a step backwards so that my hand fell to my side.

'You really hurt me, Sadie Nathanson,' he said. His eyes narrowed and this weird shiver shot through my body when he said that. I felt totally freezing. I thought about the music lab without him. I thought about the school gate without him. Tony Cruz, Photoshopped out of every situation. This blank space. Empty.

'So now you're not going to forgive *me*?' I whispered.

We were just staring at one another like we were

perfect strangers, and at that moment the sun came out from behind the low cloud and lit up the room.

I put my hand out to him again and this time he held it, and then he pulled me to him and kissed me. I felt myself warming from the inside out, the kiss cancelling out the cold chill and Tony's face coming back into focus in all of those empty scenarios. I was the luckiest girl alive. I had two bosses who thought I was worthy of their jobs, and a half-sister and a cousin who sought out my company, and I had just got my best friend and boyfriend back and that was kind of the most important thing of all.

'I am so, so sorry,' I said.

'So am I,' said Tony Cruz.

I felt like he meant it. Sure, he'd seen me at my worst – selfish, mistaken, pig-headed. But he still liked me. He still wanted me.

And we hugged. And while we hugged I tucked the label into the back of his pants and I did it so that he never even noticed. And then the hug turned into another kiss, and just as the kiss was about to turn into some proper TLC the doorbell rang and it was my cousin Billy on the doorstep.

'Hi,' said Billy, and he sighed.

I left them there, my boyfriend and my cousin. They were talking guitars. I knew that Tony would never mention how hurt he was to Billy and I knew that Billy would never apologise, but as long as they were talking guitars then everything would be OK. I headed over to Aunt Lilah's blinded by tears of relief and trying to think of a plausible explanation as to why I was a whole hour early.

In the event she didn't require one. She just looked about as grateful as it's possible for a hairdresser to look when she has a perm in one chair and a straightening in the other, and someone's grandchild standing on the shop counter singing 'Jesus Wants Me for a Sunbeam'.

I went into the back room and pulled on my tabard.

'Brrrrush!' I said as I stepped out into the salon.

Somehow in all of this chaos I had become a total pro.

27

Sadie Nathanson: Hairdressing Machine

Final preparation for the trainee hairdresser (or barber) entering the competition should be about putting together all the elements learned during the apprenticeship and at college sessions, and putting these into time-limited practice. The ability to work efficiently within time is extremely important to the preparation work for the competition day.

Guideline 27: Thames Gateway Junior Apprentice Hairdresser (or Barber) of the Year Award

For the three weeks leading up to the competition I buried myself in my art.

I put Tony on restricted contact hours and I thought of doing the same for Billy for a split second, except that there was no need. Billy had more or less dropped out of my world overnight. He was rehearsing after school every day with Interpol.

'I am actually worried about his studies for the first time ever,' Aunt Lilah confided in me one afternoon while we were cleaning up and sweeping the floor left to right as you're facing the back door, etc. 'He'll fall behind, and it's one of his most important years – he's got to get good grades or he won't end up with that university place he's been chasing ever since he could spell the word PhD.'

I kind of admired Billy's dedication to the God of Electric-Guitar-Playing. He was also clocking up the coolness points at school, which I hoped might rub off on me. People were starting to mention the new band he'd joined, which apparently had more cred than Rock Dove. They'd even had some reviews on music websites.

Marie had texted me the other day about it.

Marie: Is Billy in band Interpol?
SD: Yep
Marie: Coooooool Fabtastick!

The word for Marie was definitely 'perky'. I showed Aunt Lilah the text.

'That girl is always so sweet and sunny,' she said. 'I guess some people have naturally "up" personalities. I wish I could be more like that. I'd love to be a sunny person.'

'But you are, my love!' Uncle Zé's voice boomed from outside the back door. 'You are my little ray of sunshine!'

Aunt Lilah sighed and leaned on the sink she was wiping. She couldn't have looked less like a little ray of sunshine. We were united in our unperkiness.

'I don't think we do sunny and upbeat, do we?' I said. I felt suddenly closer to her, which was an odd feeling to have about my Aunt Lilah.

'Nah.' She smiled at me. 'We do grim determination.'

We were *experts* in grim determination. After all, wasn't I still clinging on here hoping to win that competition I'd been working for forever? Maybe others would have fallen by the wayside given the obstacles I'd had to negotiate: Aunt Lilah, Dariusz, Dariusz-and-Enrico, Tony, Tony-and-Billy and Aimée Price.

Aimée Price.

To be fair, Aimée Price had attempted something approaching an apology herself at college.

'It was just meant to be a joke, honestly – I just changed the temperature, that's all I did,' she said. 'It just went a bit, y'know, out of control.'

'Yes, it did rather,' I said. 'I lost my job.'

I said it without expression. I wanted to make her as uncomfortable as possible.

'I honestly didn't know he'd fired you until a few days later when I was telling Tony about it and he told me. So of course I went straight round there . . .'

I listened to Aimée Price rewriting history, putting herself at the centre as usual, and I thought to myself, *Girl you are about as smart as bait – did you never think I'd go and check out your story with the original source?*

'Anyway,' she said, 'at least I managed to get you your job back.'

'Yes,' I said, deadpan again. 'So you did. Thanks for that.'

I was the Ice Queen. I was marble. I was impervious to outside forces. Until that competition day, nobody was going to rattle me. Especially not Aimée Price.

And then Marie told me she wanted to come and watch me in the competition – and I was well and truly rattled.

'So I want to come and support you on the Big Day! Can I just rock up? Do I need a ticket?'

She was so keen and so, well, perky.

'I think you pay on the door,' I said. I tried to make my voice sound more sunny, but Marie made me feel really colourless sometimes. 'But there's really no need, I don't expect anyone to sit through a boring hair competition.'

It hadn't occurred to me that anyone would want to come and watch me.

'But I want to! 'Marie squeaked. 'I feel like I was there when you entered it so now I want to see it through to its conclusion! I expect your family will be there too. Maybe Abe would want to come – and how about Sarah?'

'I hadn't thought about it,' I said. 'I haven't invited them or anything. I'll send you the details, but really, Marie, nobody has to come. Unless you're truly interested in hairdressing it will be about as riveting as a box of Kirby grips.'

Please, please don't come. Don't come to watch me quite possibly fall flat on my face. In public.

'Wouldn't miss it for anything!' said Marie.

'I hope you're not expecting me to be at your competition,' said Dariusz.

'You don't *do* competitions,' I said.

'That's correct, and it's also being held on a Monday and I have my ordering to do on a Monday.'

I knew all about the ordering and I knew it took a maximum of ten minutes to do. Not that I minded whether or not Dariusz was at the competition. Except maybe it might have provided me with some inspiration, seeing him sitting there with that freaky expression on his face – that look of utter contempt which apparently means he's impressed with you. Him and Aunt Lilah. Actually, I secretly hoped that they might both turn up. The two opposing ends of my hairdressing world.

'Of course, I'd love to come on Monday,' said Aunt Lilah. 'But as you know, the salon is open and it'll be chockers.'

'Sure,' I said, leaning on my broom.

'My thoughts will be with you though, love, I will have everything crossed. You deserve it. If anyone's worked hard, it's been you.'

Did I ever think I'd hear Aunt Lilah saying those words? Maybe that was enough. Maybe she didn't need to actually be there.

But still, it might have been nice if she'd said she'd come.

28

The Heat

Although this is an individual's competition, hairdressing salons by their nature are team organisations, so even though you will be working alone on the day of the competition, the judges will be looking at the way you work with the client as well as paying careful attention to your lecturer's statement regarding your team skills.

Guideline 28: Thames Gateway Junior Apprentice Hairdresser (or Barber) of the Year Award

This was it. This was the day I'd been waiting for. Working for. Forever.

'You are going to do just fine,' said Tony Cruz.

He kissed me hard as we stood in the car park of my building. A regular snogfest while Enrico waited patiently in the car.

'When you and my brother have finished eating one another then we could actually leave,' shouted Enrico, smiling at me through the window so that my knees went weak – even though I knew for certain now that his smiles were for friendship and nothing more.

I squeezed Tony's hand, got in the car and fastened my seatbelt and we were off.

The Thames Gateway Junior Apprentice Hairdresser (or Barber) of the Year Award was being held in the Riverside Shopping Centre, which was somewhere in Kent. The organisers had roped off the central atrium of the steel-and-glass structure and constructed a huge podium at one end of the mall. On top of the podium was a long table, sporting a banner that said *Welcome to the Thames Gateway Junior Apprentice Hairdresser (or Berber) of the Year Award* – which made it sound as if it was a competition to find the best hairdresser or person of North African origin.

I fumbled in my bag and pulled out my 'Details of the Day' timetable. This was to be a knockout tournament consisting of two rounds: the first round would be simple styling (washing, blow-dry, hair up, etc.) and the final would be a total restyle. The final also boasted 'celebrity clients'.

Celebrities? At the Riverside Shopping Centre? It seemed unlikely.

There were two hundred hairdressers packed into the Riverside Shopping Centre that morning. Behind the podium table sat the judging panel – an even split of men and women who presumably ran their own successful hairdressing empires, but none of whom had bothered to spell-check the banner they were sitting behind.

Below the stage were the workstations. Two hundred in all. Each had a chair and a sink and an array of products and tools. The air was filled with the sound of shrieking, the smell of lacquer and a haze of fake tan. Somewhere among the two hundred was Aimée Price.

'Ladies and gentlemen!' came an announcement over the loud speakers. One of the competition judges was speaking. 'Welcome to the Thames Gateway Junior Apprentice Hairdresser (or Barber) of the Year Award!'

These people were so hyped up that I reckon they would've applauded a baby filling its nappy or an old lady showing her bus pass, because the most ear-splitting cheer went up from the crowd.

Of course, as often happens in crowd scenes where there is an excess of enthusiasm, somebody over-clapped. It came from the spectator seats to the left of the workstations. As I turned and looked I saw with amazement that it was Marie.

'Sadieeeee! Woooo! Go Sadieeeeee!'

I smiled at her and shrugged and then turned back to face the stage, pretending that this had nothing to do with me and that I was not actually Sadie. The only thing that betrayed me was the blush that crept up the back of my neck and bled into my cheeks. I could feel my face radiating heat.

'Jeez,' whispered Tony, nodding his head, 'you have a fan!'

'She's enthusiastic,' said Enrico, looking over in Marie's direction.

Marie waved at us. We waved back.

'That's right,' I said. 'That's my half-sister Marie. She's perky.'

'In a moment, people, we're going to be putting you through your paces,' continued the judge. 'So just be patient while our markers walk among you and brief you on what's going to happen this morning. Spectators are asked to make their way to their seats for now.'

A hand touched my elbow. I swung round and saw Florence heading for her seat.

'Good luck!' she mouthed at me.

'Good luck . . .' Tony whispered in my ear. 'Go get 'em.'

'Brrrrush.'

My head was a wash, blow-dry and hair up. This was going to be a nice simple manoeuvre to begin with. The model, Sonia, had an oval face, so she would suit anything. Unfortunately, she had also been on a photographic shoot the day before and her hair was full of gunk.

'Really sorry about the state of it,' she said while I was washing it in water that was not too hot or too cold. 'They used this sort of glue on it – plastered it down to my head.'

'So they did!' I said brightly, as little clumps of molten plastic floated to the surface. Throughout the three separate shampoos I had to apply, I was feeling the model's head, half-closing my eyes and trying to channel a hairstyle that would suit her, and that she wanted but perhaps did not know she wanted.

'I'm afraid that Sonia's hair took three washes,' I

explained to the marking judge who was observing my heat.

'Hmmm,' she said. 'I noticed that you were rather . . . painstaking with the washing. A little slow perhaps.'

I was out of the competition. I was so out of it.

'But you recovered well,' she said briskly, marking her sheet with what looked like a tick if you were looking at it upside down.

Back in. Back in. I was still in with a chance.

And I really had recovered well. Sonia had wanted a classic bride chignon. I mean, she'd actually *requested* a chignon – a chignon! How much did I love Aunt Lilah now? Of course it wasn't simple; Sonia's hair was all different lengths and so it required a million pins, which I had to hide in the hair so that she didn't end up like a porcupine. All the while I thought of Dariusz breathing down my neck. '*You've missed a bit . . . missed a bit,*' I could hear him say. '*Don't leave that strand loose – gather it up, that's it, jam it down – a chignon is neat, it's sophisticated – it's French goddammit – those women have style. Now do it again. And again. And again. And again.*'

There was a box of hair spirals at my workstation and I liberally sprinkled diamante chips throughout the 'do. Sonia looked neat, sophisticated, romantic. She looked like a bride.

'Lovely, dear, lovely,' said the judge.

'Woooo Sadie!' Marie again, whooping at me from the spectators' gallery.

I glanced up because I just couldn't help myself, and I saw a row of people that made my heart stop beating for one second. There, in the same place and at the same time, were, in order: Sarah, Abe, Marie, Billy, Tony, Mum, Aunt Lilah, Uncle Zé, Enrico, Great Aunty Rita and Dariusz.

The sight of Aunty Rita sandwiched between Enrico and Dariusz nearly finished me off, although Aunty Rita and Dariusz appeared to be deep in conversation with one another. What had they found to talk about? As I glanced in their direction Marie shouted something to the row and they all obediently raised these little white placards, which read:

COMEONSADEI

I gasped. It was slightly surreal to see my family, friends and employers united in something where

I – rather than, say, fried food – was the common denominator. This was probably how it feels on your wedding day when you stand in a room full of people from the remotest corners of your life and go, *Oh yeah – they're all here for me*. I'd always hated that idea – it seemed so attention-seeking – and yet here I was almost basking in the attention and trying not to laugh at the fact that Aunty Rita had clearly plonked herself in between Enrico and Dariusz and mucked up Marie's entire 'Go Sadie!' placard design, as well as Dariusz's chance to sit next to Enrico.

'Well done, everybody!' One of the judges was standing on the podium again. 'The standard this year has been extremely high – we believe that so far this has been our most impressive competition to date.'

A huge whoop from the crowd, and this time I didn't bother to resist. I was carried along on a wave of good feeling. I joined right in and whooped with the best of them.

'Sadly you can't all be winners,' said the judge.

We all booed and I could feel somebody's hand on my shoulder. I turned and found myself face to face with Aimée Price.

Of course, someone had to spoil my day. Aimée Price was dressed from head to toe in frosted pink. Even her hair had streaks of it. You had to admire the sheer nerve to go out like that in public. She had her fingers crossed in front of her. 'For both of us,' she mouthed at me.

'I will read out a list of surnames,' continued the judge. 'These will be our twenty finalists today.'

The list was alphabetical and as he got to 'Lamu, Christina,' I could feel my body tense.

'Lamu, Christina.' A huge cheer and an 'Omigod!' shriek.

'Martin, Drew.' Another cheer.

'Nathanson, Sadie.'

It sounded like the place had exploded. Out of the corner of my eye I could see Marie leading everyone in a chant of 'Say-dee Say-deee!'

My family, friends and employers were doing a sort of Mexican wave thing with the placards.

'Price, Aimée,' said the judge.

There was almost silence. I heard Florence in the distance give a small, polite cheer and before I knew it I was joining in. Jumping up and down – patting her on the back.

'My nan couldn't make it,' Aimée whispered to me, as if the lack of a cheering entourage needed an explanation. A line of mascara made its way down her cheek.

'Well, me and Florence are here,' I said, putting my hand on her arm, and realising in an instant just how incredibly lucky I was.

29

The Final

The judges will give points for creativity, working with the client, team skills, tidiness, efficiency, technique and timing. Competitors must aim to finish their client's hair within time.

Guideline 29: Thames Gateway Junior Apprentice Hairdresser (or Barber) of the Year Award

The final countdown.

'Girls and boys!' boomed the head of the judging panel, 'Finalists! We have a surprise for you.'

The crowd woooed, pantomime style.

'Your models for this afternoon's final will be some very familiar faces.'

More woo-wooing.

Aimée Price gripped on to my arm like I was a life buoy or something. 'Omigod,' she whispered. 'What are they going to get us to do now?'

'We said we'd have celebrities for you!' boomed the judge. 'And we do! Models – please make your way to the stage. Let's give them all a round of applause!'

Up they came: an array of eighteen people I had never seen before in my life and, among them, Misty and Dariusz. Good God! Celebrities? They wanted us to style our own bosses!

'Help!' said Aimée.

'Finalists! Please come and get your clients!'

I took a deep breath and closed my eyes, just conscious of my chest rising and falling and the breathing through my nose. I tried to shut out the whooping and screaming that was going on around me. Then I opened my eyes and walked slowly and deliberately towards the podium to where Dariusz was standing.

He was, as usual, completely expressionless.

Brrrrush.

'Good afternoon, sir,' I said, gliding across the floor with grace and poise. 'Would you like to come with me?'

Someone with a mark sheet and a clipboard was standing by. I saw her scribble something on the paper. Already.

Dariusz jumped down off the podium and followed me towards my workstation.

I gowned him and sat him down in front of the mirror.

'Now then, Mr Zengelis . . .' I was being polite and formal. After all, this was a new client and he didn't look the type who would like me to address him by his first name just yet.

'Call me Dariusz,' said Dariusz and he smiled at me. I was reminded of the first time I'd met him, when I told him that I knew Enrico and he'd attempted this smile which was kind of scary as he sort of clenched his teeth with the sheer effort of it.

'Dariusz,' I said, 'what would you like me to do for your hair today?'

I scooped up his hair in my hands. As usual it was slicked down close to his head, but now I saw that it had length and movement. There were endless possibilities with this hair.

Dariusz stared into the mirror. 'My only requirement is that you get rid of this grey here in the parting. I don't like to draw attention to my ears either, but apart from this, you can try what you like. Go mad, Sadie!'

If this was any other client then I would think *Easy peasy lemon squeezy* — after all, his requirements were modest, he had plenty of hair and there was room for total freedom and creativity in this brief. But he wasn't just any old client. This was Dariusz, and I knew that if I got it wrong he would not be able to contain himself. Even on this day of all days. He would give me a look with the pits of doom and I would know that he hated it. I had to get it right. I looked at his face shape: triangular. Why did it have to be triangular? I tried to remember what Dariusz had said about this shape. You needed to narrow the forehead area and widen the chin. It was similar to heart-shaped in women; fringe swept to the side.

I put my hands through his hair. This was where I did my channelling. While I massaged, I tilted my head back slightly and let my fingers do the work, all the while channelling — channelling the hairstyle . . . What did he want? I steadied my fingers, trying to stop the shaking by relaxing my hands. Letting the client's head massage my hands. What did he like? I had absolutely no idea what Dariusz liked.

And then it came to me. Enrico — he liked Enrico.

If he liked Enrico, then there was a good chance that he liked Enrico's hair too. But did it cover his ears and would it suit a triangular face? I glanced over to the spectator's gallery, not wanting to catch Marie's eye in case she produced some pompoms or worse. I mean, don't get me wrong, I was touched by Marie's enthusiasm – I loved that she'd managed to transform my family, friends and employer into a cheerleading team, but the 'Go Sadie!' bit just didn't sit that comfortably with me.

Luckily Marie was engrossed in conversation with Billy; animated – her entire body in an open stance turned towards him. My eyes shifted to Enrico and his hair. Fringe, tousled, tapered at the nape, brushed forward, ears covered. It would do for Dariusz. He could wear it. He might not even hate it.

'OK,' I said brightly, smiling into the mirror and trying to pretend that it wasn't my boss staring back at me out of the black pits of doom. My worry crinkle was spreading across my forehead. I tried to ignore it. 'I think we're going to be brave here . . .'

'Good! Good!' said Dariusz, all fake enthusiasm.

'We're going to get rid of the grey and the slicked-down look. I'm going for a fringe, something tousled.

You have some fabulous natural movement and body in your hair – we should make the most of this – and we'll keep the ears covered.'

'Sounds OK,' said Dariusz.

'Would you like any colour, other than getting rid of the grey?'

'Like I say, Sadie – go mad!'

And then I decided on the genius stroke: I would pick out the tips with low-lights. The feathered bits would be red-gold, avoiding the ears so we didn't draw attention to them, but going for the tips of his fringe. Just a few foils would do it, and semi-permanent on the grey.

I went for it.

'We're going to go for this colour on your grey.' I held up the chart so that Dariusz and the marker could see that it was a dead ringer for the client's original shade. 'And then we're going for Tangerine Gold on the tips!'

I waited for Dariusz to scream 'Noooooooooooo!', but he just pulled his lips back over his teeth and practised that manoeuvre known as a grin. Terrifying.

I began.

I mixed. I tore. I painted. I folded neatly, making each

crease a little work of art. I looked around the room, noticing that Dariusz was one of the few males having his hair done. Those with male bosses had a distinct advantage. Far less hair. I was going to be through with this client in good time.

I could see Aimée working on Misty and I felt for her. Her boss's hair had finally come out of the scrunchie, but you could see why she kept it there. Misty's hair was a disaster zone; even from here I could see it was in terrible condition, an evil colour of tortoiseshell where the grey ran through deep brown. You would want to cut it all off and start again. Aimée looked cheerful enough though.

I put Dariusz under the lights, checking and double-checking the thermostat.

I left him for forty minutes while I tidied up my workstation. Swept up – although we hadn't got to the cutting yet – unblocked my sink, lined up my combs and scissors. Then I had another stroke of genius. I picked up my broom and I went beyond my workstation. Around some of the empty ones. After all, this is what you did in the salon, wasn't it? You didn't just tidy up after yourself. I couldn't be seen to be sitting down reading a copy of *Hello*.

And so I swept, and while I swept I relaxed and stole a glance at my family and friends, who looked as if they were about to die of boredom. You had to love them really! I had warned Marie, but they'd come anyway; Aunty Rita was dozing, her head resting on Enrico's shoulder, her mouth wide open. She was probably snoring. Marie was still turned towards Billy. Meanwhile, Billy and Tony were talking intently. This was a good sign. I wondered for a brief, deluded moment if they were telling each other how hurt they'd felt, how betrayed, how sorry they were that things had got so complicated. But the reality was that they were probably just talking about which Gretsch they wanted next or whether Enrico had fixed the turbo yet. But hey – as long as they were talking I was happy with it.

Only Mum and Aunt Lilah remained resolutely fixed on what I was doing. Aunt Lilah was leaning right forward in her seat, staring intently at me.

The timer went and I took the lights off Dariusz, led him to the sinks and removed the foils, and then back to my now gleaming workstation. Now for the difficult bit. The actual cut.

Snip. Snip. The length was gone at the back. I tapered to the nape. I sculpted around the ears. I feathered the fringe. The tips had come out nicely.

And then I saw it. Right at the back towards the bottom of Dariusz's head. A small round patch of white. One of those weird, inexplicable patches that some men get. A patch that screamed 'STRESSS!' It must have been hidden beneath the long strands of slicked-down hair.

The marker spotted it too.

'Wow,' I said, 'how interesting.' I was trying to be calm, but all the while my heart was leaping out of my chest. 'You have a slightly different colour in this piece of hair,' I said. 'A much lighter colour.'

'Really?' said Dariusz. 'Let me see.'

I held up the mirror.

'Oh dear,' he said. 'It must have been hidden.'

'It was,' I said.

There was a temptation to just snip it out, but it would completely ruin the line. If there was one thing that Dariusz had taught me, it was how to do a job properly. Hadn't he made me tear the foils fifty times to get a straight line? There was no question of cutting corners. I would have to dye the patch. I would have to re-mix the colour, get the foil out, the lights – all for this one rogue patch of white.

I looked around. Misty was still under the lights, but who knew how much time we had left?

There was no question. I would have to re-do the 'do.

'I'm sorry, Dariusz,' I said, 'but I'm going to have to dye the back here to get rid of that patch.'

Dariusz did not look up from his magazine. 'You do what you have to do, Sadie,' he said.

So I did what I had to do. I mixed, I foiled and I put him back under the lights, and while he was under there I could see everyone finishing up and cleaning their workstations and my client was still under the goddam lights.

'You should be finishing up now, guys and gals!' said the lead judge, mounting the podium.

I could see my family and friends leaning forward in their seats. Aunt Lilah kept looking at me and then at her watch.

'You should be finishing up,' my marker said to me. She smiled wanly at me. She felt sorry for me. I felt sorry for me too.

I still had ten minutes under the lights for Dariusz. I turned the thermostat up – going for a more speedy finish – and I watched him like a hawk for signs of smoke. Then I raced, broom in hand, around my workstation, piles of hair in the bin, sink cleaned and worktop polished.

Lights up, foil off, head washed and client gowned and in chair ready for drying – and then the buzzer went and it was all over. And I had failed because I hadn't finished.

And it was a disaster.

30

The Thames Gateway Junior Apprentice Hairdresser (or Barber) of the Year Award

We are used to drama in the salon and the competition will be no exception. No doubt there will be some unusual and surprising situations and we hope that, rather than discouraging competitors, these will test and challenge them, making them perform to the very best of their abilities.

Guideline 30: Thames Gateway Junior Apprentice Hairdresser (or Barber) of the Year Award

The 'celebrities' stood on the stage in a line. Every single one of them preened and coiffed.

Except my client.

Dariusz Zengelis stood with a towel wrapped around his shoulders, while moisture dripped down his forehead. He dabbed vaguely at it while practising grinning.

'Oh dear!' said one of the judges, 'I see somebody ran out of time!'

I was *so* in last place.

To calm myself I pretended to be Miss Frame. I breathed in and out slowly. I put my hand on my chest and felt it rise and fall. But it rose and fell rather too quickly. I was gulping in panicky little breaths. So then I distracted myself by trying to decide whether or not this experience was the most humiliating in my life to date. I thought that it probably was. After all, it was happening in front of two hundred hairdressers, not to mention all my friends and family and my college lecturer, and what felt like a bazillion other complete strangers.

'What the hell happened to you?' said Aimée. 'I thought you were finishing hours ahead of everyone else when I looked over.'

'I missed a bit of white – just showed up when I trimmed at the end.'

'Couldn't you cut it out? I'd have cut it out!' said Aimée.

'I guess I could've, but I tried to think what I'd do in a salon. You wouldn't cut it out, would you? You'd do

263

it properly, even if it took twice as long. Which it did.'

'S'bad luck, hey?'

I looked up at Misty. She was transformed. Hair all grey-blonde, one colour. No scrunchie in sight.

'You did a great job, Aimée,' I told her, because it was true.

She smiled. 'Thanks,' she said and squeezed my arm with her frosted pink acrylics.

The judges convened with their clipboards. I could see my marker leaning over and speaking animatedly to the others. She was gesturing towards Dariusz. The other judges were raising their eyebrows. One of them looked over at me.

Eventually the lead judge rose, firstly to a huge cheer and then to a hush that descended over the audience. Quite a feat in itself.

'We have reached our decision,' said the judge. 'It's been a difficult competition this year, but we feel that our decision is fair and, of course, final.'

The crowd took a breath in. All except me. I didn't need to because mine was the only client who wasn't finished. Dariusz still stood dripping at the front of the stage.

'In third place . . .' said the judge. 'For client transformation, listening to instruction and finishing within time – is Aimée Price from Cissor's Palace in East London!'

Misty jumped up and down on the stage, and Aimée herself gripped my arm so tightly I thought she was going to pull it off.

'Go up! Go up!' I whispered.

Aimée staggered, all frosted pink and matching, up on to the stage, where she received a kiss and an envelope and a small trophy. She looked as if she was going to pitch head-first off the stage. It was a pity her nan wasn't there to see this.

'We have no second place,' said the judge.

'Huh?' said over two hundred people collectively.

'We have no second place. What we have is a tie for first place, and I will have to explain why.'

I was tempted to tune out. After all, there was no reason for me to even be here now. Couldn't I just escape via the fire exit?

'For a superb creative cut-and-colour and efficiency in finishing the client on time – first place goes to Sandra Dawn of Jam, Southend!'

The crowd went wild. Including me. It was a release of tension, as well politeness and sudden hairdresser camaraderie. Sandra Dawn's client revealed herself by jumping up and down and whooping along. It was a truly great cut, really creative, a zig-zag parting in a Cleopatra style with purple detail. A dream really.

'Now,' said the judge when the crowd had quietened down again, 'I'm going to say one word that I don't expect any of you to be familiar with: Poliosis.'

We all looked blankly at one another.

'Poliosis is a mysterious patch of white in the hair, which some clients have and which sometimes we don't realise they have . . . until it's too late.'

I saw Dariusz's head jerk upwards and that strange, slow grin spread across his face.

OMIGOD. Poliosis. Patch of white. It was Dariusz. Which meant that it was me. They were talking about me.

'First place for an excellent style and colour, but most importantly for absolutely refusing to take the short way round and for ensuring that the client got the best possible service, and for almost finishing on time, in spite of the set-back – joint first place goes to Sadie Nathanson of Stylee Stylee, Roman Road.'

And then the room went black.

I came round to a St John Ambulance person smiling in my face. Aunt Lilah was holding my hand and Dariusz was fanning me with a copy of *Heat,* his hair still dripping gently down his face. He pointlessly wiped the drips away.

'Well, good grief!' said Aunt Lilah as she came into focus. 'Sadie Nathanson – you are such a drama queen!'

'Poliosis,' I said. 'I never knew it was called that.'

I sat up, leaning into Aunt Lilah's shoulder, allowing her perfume cloud to envelop me.

'I think we all learned something here today,' said Dariusz.

My head finally stopped spinning. I sipped some water that the St John Ambulance man handed me and I felt OK. A bit drained possibly, but really I was OK.

'I'm OK,' I said. 'And I think I won. Or did I dream that bit?'

'And I came third!' There was was Aimée Price. She was standing above me as well.

They were all there. Abe, Sarah, Marie, Billy, Aunt Lilah, Mum, Aunty Rita, Uncle Zé, Enrico, Dariusz, Florence, Aimée and Tony. And they were all smiling. Tony bent over and kissed the top of my head.

'Well done, killer!' he said. 'I knew you'd do it.'

In the background I could see Uncle Zé's face looming. Even in my enfeebled state I was conscious of the fact that Tony had just kissed me and Uncle Zé had seen him. I decided to ignore it. I had seventeen chaperones here – the chances of anything happening were nil. Surely even he realised that?

'I feel like such an idiot,' I said to Tony. 'I can't believe I fainted.'

I got to my feet, leaning heavily on him.

'You are an idiot,' said Tony. 'But you're my idiot,' he whispered. 'And I love you.'

There was a sudden squealing as Marie made her way over.

'You were A-MAZING!' she said. 'We couldn't see what was going on at the end when you suddenly had to re-do your boss's hair – and we were like OMIGOD, what is going on? Why is she starting all over? We couldn't believe it and then when you won and then

268

when you fainted. OMIGOD – what an afternoon! SAYDEE! SAYDEE!'

'Yeah, well done,' said Billy, typically low-key.

'Double-triple well done,' said Abe and he smiled warmly at me.

'Good job!' said Enrico. 'Anyone who can get Dariusz to stand on the stage looking like a drowned rat is some kind of genius!' and he laughed his head off.

And Mum was there squeezing my hand, the rims of her eyes red, a mist across them. She smiled at me. 'Good girl,' she said. 'All that work is paying off.'

'Your boss is going to do my hair,' said Great Aunty Rita, peering at me. 'I'm coming into that salon of his next Saturday. He's persuaded me. It's just a try-out.'

Dariusz practised grinning again. Clearly this is what they'd been talking about. Aunty Rita had never let anyone apart from Marcello of Ilford touch her hair. Not even her own niece, who had her own salon. Mostly the hair sat rigid under an old-lady hat and it occasionally quivered when she got animated, which wasn't often. She was going to let Dariusz loose on it? Terrifying. Who knew what the result would be?

And then the judge was coming over holding an

envelope and a very large shiny trophy in the shape of a pair of scissors.

'Are we recovered?' he said. He was accompanied by my marker, who was still holding her clipboard.

'Ye-es,' I said, 'I'm really embarrassed. I'm really sorry. It just sometimes happens.'

'Well,' said the judge, 'we feel we've made just the right choice this year. Obviously there is always some drama at these events! I think last year someone's model caught fire.'

Dariusz shot me a look and then stared hard at Aimée.

'You were very unlucky,' said my marker. 'But you handled that really well and very professionally. It's exactly what you should do – it would have been very tempting to have cut the corner there, as it were, but you didn't. You remained absolutely calm.'

'You're a pro,' said the judge. 'You're lucky to have her working for you,' he said to Dariusz.

'Yes,' said Dariusz and Aunt Lilah together, 'I am.'

31

My First Paying Client

We sincerely hope that prize winners will benefit from their success in our competition. Former prize-winners have been approached by salons keen to recruit them as well as clients asking for them specifically.

Thames Gateway Junior Apprentice Hairdresser (or Barber) of the Year Award

I tried a chignon. I spritzed with spray, pulled it back into a low pony, sectioned in two and twisted it until it felt tight, wrapping it around the elastic. I wrapped the next section around the first and secured it.

I stared at the result in my bedroom mirror. Not bad. And fast too. My fringe was really growing out and I was able to smooth it back almost into the bun itself. Just a couple of Kirby grips and some spray. Cleopatra was almost gone. I was a whole new me.

I picked up my trophy from the nightstand and

held it up in front of the mirror. The golden scissors, the plaque saying 'First Prize: Thames Gateway Junior Apprentice Hairdresser (or Barber) of the Year Award'. This was just the beginning, I decided. There would be more of these. A row of trophies. And there would be my own salon with my own exclusive clients and stylish chairs and . . .

The buzzer went. Dammit. I replaced the trophy carefully, left the Kirbys on the night-stand and dived for the intercom handset. I could see Tony's face on the fuzzy black-and white-screen. Even in fuzzy black-and-white he was cute.

'Can I come up?' he said.

'I'm about to go to work!' I said.

It was Wednesday and Aunt Lilah was a stickler for punctuality – as well as sweeping in a particular direction. I needed to be there by four. It was 3.55.

'Five minutes?'

'Three!'

He was at the door in an instant.

'Is your ma in?'

'Nobody is in.'

'That can't be right,' said Tony. 'Isn't your uncle

behind the door with an axe or something?'

I checked. 'Nup. But I have to be at Aunty's in like three minutes now.'

'Can I come in?'

'Two minutes,' I said. 'You do pick your moments.'

'I like your hair.'

'I can do the same for you if you like.'

He walked over the threshold and the next thing his arms were around my waist and his mouth was kissing my neck and we held each other for the longest time. It still felt so good to have him back – even if it was only for three minutes of alone-time.

'Do you know, Sadie Nathanson, just how much you mean to me?' said Tony.

'Tell me,' I said. 'But you have to do it on the way to Delilah's or Aunty will fire me AGAIN.'

At Delilah's, Aunt Lilah was between clients. She was on the phone as I walked in, Tony's goodbye kiss still making my lips hum.

'I'll put you through to upstairs, love, hold on – Billy should pick up, he's definitely there,' said Aunt Lilah into the receiver.

She replaced the handset and raised her eyebrows at me. 'That was your Marie,' she said. 'She's rung him three times. That's all I'm saying.'

Aunt Lilah winked at me and checked the appointments book.

'Three times?' I said.

'Four times!' Uncle Zé called out from the basement of the shop. He came up the stairs.

'All right, *anak* – my prize-winner!' He came forward and kissed me. 'Marie has called him four times! It's good! My boy is a heartbreaker, like his father.'

I watched Uncle Zé go out the back door with an extra bounce in his walk and it occurred to me that if Billy had been a girl then Uncle Zé would not have been boasting about how many phone calls he'd received from an admirer. He just would've been stood on the front doorstep with an egg beater, looking menacing.

So Marie had called Billy four times? And Billy was happy to take her calls. Aunt Lilah seemed to think that there was definitely something in it, although she played it down.

'Four times. I'm not saying there's anything in it, but I know he has called her back.'

'How d'you know?'

'I just know. I'm his mother. I'm paid to know this stuff.'

So Marie was interested in Billy, was she? My geeky cousin Billy! My perky half-sister Marie! Who'd have thunk it? I couldn't wait to confront Billy. It would have to wait till the end of this shift though.

'You have a client at 4.30,' said Aunt Lilah.

'*I* have a client?' I peered at her. I didn't take clients at Delilah's, or Stylee Stylee. I swept, cleaned, unblocked sinks, did coffees, gowned up and meeted-and-greeted. I did *bits* of clients: I did 'hair up', I did foils, I did washing and blow-drying, I sectioned, I trimmed fringes. I did the bits that no one had time for. Sometimes Dariusz and Aunty watched me work. Sometimes they didn't. But I did not have clients.

'Special request, this one,' said Aunt Lilah. 'Insisted it was you and no one else. I'm out the back for a Kit Kat and a cup of tea if you need me. Which you won't.'

I checked the clock. 4.28. I had two minutes.

What to do? The shop looked tidy. There was a

temptation to just sit in one of the comfy chairs and leaf through a mag. But my feet involuntarily took me to the corner of the room where the broom lived. I picked it up and started to sweep. When you looked closely you could see that there was a ton of hair under the workstations – it sat in little pools and if it wasn't swept then when the wind came under the door it would blow it all over the shop. It was important also to make sure that you swept it from left to right as you were facing the back door, because that was the way the floor tilted, and if you swept it uphill then the wind would blow it downhill and it would go everywhere.

I made a mental note to myself to make sure that when I bought my own salon the floor wouldn't be on a tilt. I would take a spirit level with me to check, if necessary.

'Yoo-hoo! I'm here for my 4.30, dearie!' And there was Mrs Nellist calling out to me from the front door. 'I said to your Aunt Lilah that I wouldn't have anyone else. She said you got a trophy or somethink, and I said, "I'm not surprised" – you done a great job on my hair last time.'

I smiled at her. Then I whispered 'brrrrush' under my breath.

'Afternoon, Mrs Nellist – let me take your coat for you,' I said and I glided towards her.

She was my first proper paying client.

I absolutely loved her.

Have you read...?

Dads, Geeks & Blue Haired Freaks

ELLIE PHILLIPS

One girl's search for her dad
using the Internet, some boys
and quite a lot of hairspray

EGMONT PRESS: ETHICAL PUBLISHING

Egmont Press is about turning writers into successful authors and children into passionate readers – producing books that enrich and entertain. As a responsible children's publisher, we go even further, considering the world in which our consumers are growing up.

Safety First
Naturally, all of our books meet legal safety requirements. But we go further than this; every book with play value is tested to the highest standards – if it fails, it's back to the drawing-board.

Made Fairly
We are working to ensure that the workers involved in our supply chain – the people that make our books – are treated with fairness and respect.

Responsible Forestry
We are committed to ensuring all our papers come from environmentally and socially responsible forest sources.

**For more information, please visit our website at
www.egmont.co.uk/ethical**